David Mar studied English and American literature before becoming a chronicler, writer and research psychologist. He's a proud dad and a nature-lover. He has published poetry folios on various subjects ranging from isolation, grief and love to nature, spirituality and politics. His fiction work flirts with real life crimes, horror and the supernatural, where he celebrates the ordinary everyday lives that make the extraordinary possible. His recent work explores dystopia and gender identity.

To love, adventure and my daughter Amelia

David Mar

THE EVERBLUE

A Game of Shadows

AUSTIN MACAULEY PUBLISHERS™
LONDON * CAMBRIDGE * NEW YORK * SHARJAH

Copyright © David Mar 2024

The right of David Mar to be identified as author of this work has been asserted by the author in accordance with sections 77 and 78 of the Copyright, Designs and Patents Act 1988.

All rights reserved. No part of this publication may be reproduced, stored in a retrieval system, or transmitted in any form or by any means, electronic, mechanical, photocopying, recording, or otherwise, without the prior permission of the publishers.

Any person who commits any unauthorized act in relation to this publication may be liable to criminal prosecution and civil claims for damages.

This is a work of fiction. Names, characters, businesses, places, events, locales, and incidents are either the products of the author's imagination or used in a fictitious manner. Any resemblance to actual persons, living or dead, or actual events is purely coincidental.

A CIP catalogue record for this title is available from the British Library.

ISBN 9781035823697 (Paperback)
ISBN 9781035823703 (ePub e-book)

www.austinmacauley.com

First Published 2024
Austin Macauley Publishers Ltd®
1 Canada Square
Canary Wharf
London
E14 5AA

I am incredibly indebted to the Institute of Psychosynthesis, and their supportive holistic psychological training, and especially, their teaching of Dante. Thank your Rebecca for sharing your fragrant haiku and my fellow students for their spirit of acceptance. Thank you to all the staff at Ali's café. They were a source of hope, joy and inspiration during the summer of 2022. I would like to posthumously thank those authors who have inspired me to explore the genre of fantasy and the other-worldly: Edgar Allan Poe, Wilky Collins, Guy de Maupassant, and many others Bangsian artists, in other illustrious domains.

Table of Contents

After the Slaughter	11
The Raving Monk Under the Mad Moon	13
Gang Aft A-gley	18
Origan	26
A Flying Monkey	30
Dreamcast	41
Long Live Charles	45
Conspiracy	48
Epitath for a Chimpanzee	60
Plain as Plane	62
Water, Stones and Wax	65
Fishbowl Psychology	81
Little Death	93
Initiation	106
Wake's End	119
Laughter and Squealing	129
His Method of Madness	139
Night, Night …	144
The Cleansing	149
Angels of Lies	159
Acceptance	165
Six Months After the Expedition	173
Lest We Forget Walden	178
Moments of Lucidity	183

After the Slaughter

The entity was watching over her … It wasn't made of gold or plastic, but awe. Awe for the beauty of creation, with respect for the power of death over humans and the resurrection of nature.

'Glöd! Glöd!' said the priestess, as she drank from the spirit of the cave.

From the darkness of her origins, her eyes wandered to the reflection of the soft glow of the flower. Emotions crystallized in the substance of dreams, her frail beating heart seemed like a flimsy extraneous pulse. She heard her breath reverberating in the cave. Was she the only survivor?

She did not understand at first why she was lying naked, listening to this new thumping heart, at the precipice of what seemed to be a painful reversal of age. It was as if she was discovering her body for the first time.

The pain of being born, the initial gasp for air, the first lights seen through the prism of her aching eyes: she felt it all in an instant. But, without the bearings of history, she couldn't be sure her memory could be trusted, and yet she felt the whole truth of it in the moment.

She had felt her father penetrating her mother thrustfully. Was it her own conception that she had felt in that instant? Could it have been her birth she felt instead? She always knew memory loss would accompany her transformation. The entity made sure of that.

This entity could not have been her mother whose aloofness she resented so much. Yet, here she was, craving her embrace. Beatrice felt its love around her so strongly that it now felt like a sacrilege to deny it to herself.

Once she collected her thoughts, she felt a dull pain in her groin. This inguinal truth had to be revealed to the entity: an oily leakage oozing from the core of the earth was seeping into her bones:

'Mother,' she hurled, 'I have survived the slaughter!'

It is not until several few damp fires later that she understood why they had all killed each other, as if their frenzied acts had been the natural and salvatory end to her protracted nightmare. She blamed the Everblue at first, but then recanted her testimony at the witness box of some half-conscious doomsday trial presided over only by conifers and beeches.

This pain she felt, after her transcendental awakening, meant that her wound wouldn't heal without the knowledge of her suffering. Naturally, she felt the weight of loneliness and sorrow slowly lifting from her chest. She had to tell the tale …

She saw herself walking further into the forest and ancient coppices of conifers that stood proudly erect against the misty morning sky. It was only the beginning of her nurturing journey-work under an overhead gaseous ocean of green and blue. Her head lying on the moss, her eyes looking upward, she saw the earth upside down. She looked at her skin. It was covered with a sticky substance that was fragrant of flowers. She licked her lips: it tasted of pollen.

Weeks passed until she was able to truly regain control of her limbs. At the mouth of the cave, she contemplated the walk she had dreamt. She glanced backwards at the tit that had enabled her survival: a rivulet and a dripping rock still spurting with fresh limpid life. Only now, would she finally be able to walk back into the free world.

She ventured on her legs, which felt woolly under her weight at first. The mother in her, the mother to be, dignifyingly dressed with branches of Sitka spruce and bark, finally found the superhuman force to head towards civilisation again. She had pictured this forest trail in her dreams: her wounded feet covered in mulch and moss, the benevolent presence of nature around her, the fruition of her sex. Everything around her reminded her of her vegetal self.

In a clearing, as she watched the reflection of her hair in the roaring waters of a sun kissed creek, she felt glad she hadn't been eaten, now closer to reconciling her survivor's anger with the thought of a welcoming earth where the taste of hand-grabbed fruits from generous trees felt like a homecoming …

The Raving Monk Under the Mad Moon

June, two years before, at Catherine's manor:

- 'On one of the highest mountains of Japan, somewhere in the old world of legends, there is a flower that braves the strongest winds and storms. The legend says that no monarch or princess ever compared to its timeless beauty, and that only a handful of men ever laid eyes upon it. In their memory, it remains as the brightest colour they ever saw, a flower of a hue so intensely entrancing that it shattered their consciousness. Those who were brave enough to let the flower rapture their mind have held the greatest power human kind has ever seen, their subconscious revealed, their mind sublimated to realms never conquered before … At least, it's what I gathered from the monk, master Khul. Some call him a lunatic, a raving mad eccentric, others a Saint … What can I say? He went on to build his own cult. He alone knows the location of the flower.'

Charles Dubois smoothed his moustache pensively with his index finger: he realized that everything he had just told her had been entirely dictated to him by an extraneous power. Would he tell Catherine Hallmark that he was among those few anointed ones who had approached the legendary flower? God knows he wanted to. "But not now," seemed to whisper a headless voice.

Catherine, who was leaning on the edge of her seat, looked at his steepled hands as he carefully joined his fingertips in an effort to compose himself. Catherine dubitatively observed Dubois making geometrical shapes with his knuckles.

- 'Positively fantabulomagicalistic!' said Catherine enthusiastically.

There was no doubt Catherine had theatrical ways about her. Dubois attributed that uncertain fluidity in her movements that seemed to linger in aesthetic limbo to the fact she had been a dancer at the cabaret. One of the techniques she had learnt to gain power over men of vision was to butter up their fantasies with ironic deflation. It put her adversaries on their toes, and her friends, into indebtedness forever. The latter were often mesmerised into believing honesty was her weapon of choice.

As the wise, seasoned traveller she had imagined he was, Dubois incarnated his age with gusto. But as a man of taste, his clothes of vegetal origin like the wool of his mohair, the cotton of his socks and the silk of his three-piece linen suit lining, all redounded to some acquired pedigree. Besides, Dubois remained intentionally evasive about the location of the flower despite Catherine's skilful mettle:

- 'The scientific name of that flower has yet to be decided, but I heard that the monks of Tomurauchi called it the "Everblue",' said Dubois.
- 'I need a bit more than a monograph, dear Charles,' said Catherine prosaically. 'If the flower, just by looking at it, does expand your consciousness as you say, what does it feel like to smell it? That's what I would like to know. Did you stick your nose that far?' Catherine sneered.

Dubois shook his head in disbelief. He could see through her mundane antiques now. But he had yet to find a sponsor for his expedition. He could not conscionably tell her the whole story now that she was humouring him. How he had not just approached the flower but held it in his fingers was definitely not for the great Catherine's ears.

In the wooden yew chair that she had rummaged from some antiques show, he saw Catherine shirk a pang of vanity. And yes, he had distinctly experienced the flower in the very spot where Master Khul saw it the first time.

- 'But, as in all legends, where there is smoke, there is fire, I suppose,' mellowed Catherine.
- 'Oh, I am more than willing to prove it to you,' said Dubois, with aplomb and mysteriousness, 'I am a man of science, if that wasn't clear enough. But I didn't just come here today to gain your financial support for the

expedition once more, no, no. This time, I do intend to bring the seeds of that flower back, Mrs. Hallmark, mark my words!'

Catherine sat back in her own garden chair and sighed …

- 'Not this time, I am afraid Charles … I need more than hearsay testimonies, these days. Why didn't you bring the monk with you?
- But the monk belongs to his spiritual palace, Mrs. Hallmark! What would a Japanese recluse monk do in bloody Scotland? Besides, he lives by the flower,' said Dubois curtly.
- 'Couldn't you find it again on your own, that flower, or distil its power somehow?
- I … recognize your true Scottish spirit, Mrs. Hallmark, but I am afraid it can't be done. And yes, with Master Khul's help, I travelled to the flower's sanctuary, high up on Tomurauchi mountain, but he made sure that I was under his spell before guiding me to the forbidden heights, in complete trance, that is.
- Fascinating, but tell me more about him, that Mr. Cool …
- Him or her, Mrs. Hallmark … To this day, I couldn't tell.
- Do please explain, Charles, and call me Ms., I am a widow, you know.
- So you are willing to at least listen, er … Ms. Hallmark?
- Well, obviously,' said Catherine, shrugging her shoulders. 'And how did you come about this monk-friend of yours?'

Dubois characteristically brushed his pencilled moustache with his index finger and the same enigmatic sneer. He explained how his team of anthropologists had elected an ancient mountainous land on the island of Hokkaido, the land of the Ainu people, as their field of study. The monk, who had journeyed north up the trails of the Forbidden Mountain —only so called to deter tourists from the sacred and sinuous trails— had got lost in a thick blizzard. He had followed the maps taught by his ancestors, who famously never wrote down anything on paper and taken a forbidden path, disregarding the advice of his hierarchy, when he found himself surrounded by the most beautiful creation he had ever seen, the radiance of which was mind-transcending enough to warrant his subsequent seclusion.

- 'The mind is pure illusion, Ms. Hallmark ... It can only see a tiny portion of this world! What we call reality is in fact an imaginary construct. The flower has the capacity to transform brain waves into actionable information before it even reaches your faculties. 90% of our brain is out there, you see ... It's only limited by our fear of material death! And let me tell you about the monk, Ms. Hallmark: it wasn't chance but destiny that led the monk to me. He had to show me a thing or two about the mind, you see. It's time things changed. Imagine the implications for our world. Aren't current events a repeat of the same old tune?' pleaded Dubois.
- 'But is it possible that the flower was just a product of the monk's imagination?' Catherine asked sagaciously.
- 'How discerning of you, Ms Hallmark! To be able to create, you need to conceive, indeed,' said Dubois shrewdly, flapping his hands in the air as he could see his tale about the monk was slowly exerting its expected fascination on Catherine.
- 'All right, all right. Tell me about this sexless monk, then,' said Catherine.
- 'Whatever made Khul take the wrong path,' he continued, 'he heard the echo of his footsteps leaving the trail, mistaking the reverberated sound of his feet on the snow-covered trail for a spirit!'

Catherine's rounded mouth was the signal for Dubois to finally elaborate on the monk proper:

- 'One summer night, excited to show the enchanted flower to his Bhikkhu, the senior monk told him that he had followed no other trail than an ancestral path long condemned by the elders of the Tendai sect, the community of Buddhist seekers he belonged to. His admission to the sacrilege was his demise.'

Dubois went on to recall how he himself had lived in an abandoned village, after giving his Japanese guide the slip. How he had lost his way and chanced upon the dilapidated shack which the monk had elected as his retreat, deep in the forest. Dubois described how the ghost village was frozen in time, somewhere between Hiroshima and the 1970s. The first time Dubois ever saw Master Khul, he was bathing in a lake, in a clearing. The monk offered him shelter in the deserted village without a second thought. During his journey with him, which lasted several weeks, the monk led him to believe that the disconcerting sound of his echoed footsteps on the mountain path could have been the sign of a wandering spirit known by the name of "Yōkai". He believed that it was that spirit that had led him to the flower. Dubois soon learned that the monk's religious beliefs had become such a burden that he often shed off his clothes in a symbolic rebellious gesture to free himself from the shackles of his past. As they became friends, Dubois gradually witnessed how the sannyasin monk would sometimes fall prey to exhilarated spiritual fits.

- 'I did wonder if his behaviour wasn't due to PTSD from Hiroshima or the fallout of some nuclear discharge. He sometimes spoke a dialect of dubious origins. So, one night, I recorded him. I then played the monk's elucubration to my Japanese B&B host, upon my return to Tokyo, but the old lady couldn't make sense of it. Nevertheless, he opened areas of my soul I had never explored before. A whole new world opened to me. I saw my own death and travelled extraordinary lengths into what psychologists call the collective unconscious. It's deliciously mind-blowing to know how one dies. What if you could comprehend everything about your life in an instant!' said Dubois.
- 'Jonathan would be a great help to you. I'm sure of that now,' said Catherine.
- 'Who's Jonathan?
- My nephew, he's a psychiatrist. He will no doubt be helpful in the darkness of this matter,' said Catherine.

Gang Aft A-gley

- 'I wish this moment would last forever …What if forever was now?' he had said to Eleanor, looking into her eyes with more love than the world could contain.

The tranquil little town of Eden Borough was only a few miles away. But out there in the countryside, it felt like another world altogether. Jonathan used to find its market street tantalizing, with its cobbled streets and gentle sloping alleys bordered by rows of stone houses exuding with vibrant life. The neat little paintings, as many vanishing points of nostalgia, nattily exposed in the shops and galleries, spoke of the town's here and now as many frontispieces of humble happiness. The shops of the high streets Eleanor and him used to rummage through were bustling with curious interlopers and the excitement of socialisation among the audible gossip, banter and running commentaries of every day life. The roasting chickens from the butcher's, the lavender soaps from the well-being shop, the coffee aromas winnowing through the café's ventilation system out onto summer terraces; the eyes and the mouth of humanity tainted with the juggernaut of envy and carefree selfishness running wild … Jonathan felt his love-filled memories of his late wife wholly dragging his soul in their wake.

The dry roaring fire in the large hearth bringing still moisture to Jonathan Deadstone's eyes as he watches the fantastic shapes of the fire surround's gargoyles project their obfuscating and whimsical shadows on the high ceiling of his study. His mind wanders back again to January, two years before, and to the phone conversation he had with his aunt Catherine about a certain anthropologist named Dubois.

There was an entrancing music to it all then: the same flames lapping at oxygen with greed—he feels their warmth to his face even now—as the fire became the sub track for a heroic surge he hadn't felt for a long time.

Catherine has always been nuts. No doubt about that. But at the very least, he should have relied on that knowledge to extricate himself from her entrapment as soon as he had felt it. Madness is a family trait that he always fought back and he wishes now that he had not surrendered to her bipolarized view of the world so easily. Yet, he knows why he had succumbed to her stratagem: they spoke the same congenial lingo. The Hallmarks always had a reputation as entrepreneurs and philanthropists since well before the Victorian era. But their boldness didn't come without cost. A murky past impregnates their legacy. It was Catherine who best embodies the Hallmark's motto: "*mysterium tremendum et fascinans*", which loosely translated means "Fascination for terrible mystery".

A family secret always loomed over the Hallmarks like a rapacious flit flock, like a murder of whispered omens always changing shapes and tones and whose stealthy flight remains invisible. Jonathan should have known that one day or another, the idiomatic logic of the "give your dog a bad name and hang him" adage would catch up with the weakling of the family. Another scapegoating in order to preserve unity must have felt overdue, so that the Everblue expedition came in the nick of time. "If only it hadn't been at the cost of Beatrice," he deplores.

As a boy, Catherine's large athletic shoulders and her gravitas impressed Jonathan so much that he imagined she was the descendant of some headstrong Viking chieftain. The old Medusa mercilessly slashed men's pride during her spare time too perhaps. He remembers how she would inspire admiration among her *intelligenitalia*, as she would call her minions, who despite her obnoxious antiques gravitated around her. Even when his uncle was still alive, she seemed to marshal men's egos, so that they all sheepishly submitted to her whims, either through fear or cowardice. She would swoosh through the rooms of her Georgian mansion, delivering demeaning comments to her parterre of fans, and, as if to accompany her blows, would then flaunt the prerogatives of her sex in their grovelling face. Her fluid arrogance was a warhorse that left men bemused. Once, during one of her soirées, she cut short the pompous speech of a member of the Institute of Spiritual Synthesis whose name was never to be mentioned again. Jonathan always saw her as a giant sequoia towering over the rest of the humble beeches of the Hallmark family.

Lately, the shadow of Catherine Hallmark still reigned upon a decadent withered manor house since the death of her oil magnate of a husband, whom she met while a dancer. Nowadays, the dowager tended to surround herself with a motley crew of idle striplings, bibulous adventurers, TV presenters and loquacious writers whom she entertained with her framed showbiz stories. In return for their attention, they prayed on her for the sole purpose of splashing her inheritance on pie-in-the-sky projects, vicariously catching the limelight of her youthful insanity. Aunt Catherine had recently met such a gigolo. His name was Herbert. His main occupation was to keep her young, she unashamedly admitted to her daughter, Beatrice, on her 18th birthday.

As he sees the fire dying, the music of Jonathan Deadstone's inner silence turns into a tinnitus on a theme in D. If it wasn't for the wonderstruck tone in her voice that night, he would not have measured the terrible awe that recoiled from her encounter with Dubois. He had allowed her excitement to ripple through his blood so that he had ignored the ringing that was meant to alert him.

A few weeks later, Dubois was expected at his Scottish mansion. He remembers making plans to buy sake in China town. The French anthropologist, who had risked his sanity living in an abandoned mountain village with a schizoid monk, certainly deserved his attention, but had only been mentioned by passing during his phone conversation with Catherine:

- 'And you're telling me just now?' he had said, furious. 'You know I am a keen botanist! Surely, when he mentioned a sacred flower?'

She had hypocritically dismissed Dubois' elucubrations at first, only to tantalize her nephew with the prospects of a magical flower hunt later. Yet, if he had audibly perceived her perplexedness over the phone, he kept wondering what it was that Dubois really had said. He could not for the life of him trust his aunt to give him a rational account of the man's visit.

"She sure is a magnet for such extraordinary tales as Dubois," he had admitted. He was intrigued and trapped. After arranging a meeting with Dubois, he had driven off as far as he could from his Scottish den along the emerald forest of dark shaded conifers to project his bushy thoughts on the night canopy. It was then that the many agley silhouettes of light cast by the full moon had revealed their auguries. He often drove to escape wraiths of Eleanor since her passing. He could not quite explain why the existence of the mystical flower had raised his hopes that night, neither could he fully figure out why Catherine had omitted to keep him in the loop about the sacred flower.

As the spirits of the conifers that lined the dark winter landscape fed his overactive mind with some childish swashbuckling fantasies involving Japanese samurais, he had wondered whether to give the anthropologist's account a miss, but had felt compelled to meet Dubois in person. Catherine was always such a spoof, but he had to give it to her, the decadent socialite made the most interesting connections.

Once back home, he had surveyed the nocturnal garden, looking for signs of a telltale rising wind or a pre-cognitive rustle among the conifers and aspens. It was pitch black as usual around the mansion that had once belonged to a member of the MacLeod clan. Listening intently to the night, the psithurism among the trees had reminded him of one of his female patients whom he would receive in his study. That was towards the end of his career. She was obnubilated by head voices and had to listen to Stephen Fry before going to sleep for fear of becoming mad. Her case had fascinated him. Since his retirement, however, he had found it difficult to occupy his hollow solitary hours. He had bought the house to please his wife Eleanor but never felt at peace in it. Ever.

As he catches his own reflection in the bay window, Jonathan feels reassured. He sits himself deeper into his armchair. His eyes shut, he paints the picture of a dragon fly hovering over a pond and soon, his soul flies once more towards the top of the sacred Japanese mountain. Love can make you blind, but it shouldn't make you stupid. He must have imagined the monk painfully climbing the rocky face of the sacred mountain, or even heard his footsteps echoing in a parallel world while fomenting his eloping fantasy with his aunt's daughter, Beatrice. He must have identified with that monk, and the spirit walking by his side, towards the magic flower to justify travelling with her to the end of the world. Otherwise, how could he have been so incautious as to involve Beatrice in his mystical and esoteric wanderings? He had to admit it: the idea of an expedition had seeped into his mind to reconnect his forlorn soul to its lost glory through some incestuous fantasy that involved the young Beatrice.

The French anthropologist had the secret ambition to present a TV show series, all the while insisting that the Everblue should remain a secret:

'As if!' Catherine had chuckled goofily.

"As if indeed," he had thought, knowing his aunt would certainly alert the whole mediatic quadrant about the whole business in the same breath as she demeaned Dubois' tale. Dubois for that matter couldn't possibly keep the Everblue a secret, let alone Catherine!

As sure as his aspens were being walloped by the strong January winds, he resented the French adventurer had not come to him first with the story. He must have sensed, when Dubois let the cat out of the bag in Catherine's reception room, that a terrible disaster would be unleashed on the Hallmark family. If only he had listened to his reasonable self, he would have realised how his terrible qualms about gambling with Beatrice's life were justified.

He instinctively looks at the baby picture of his daughter in search of some comfort, marvelling at the delicate colour of her rosy cheeks. He has not heard from her since Beatrice's disappearance. Is it karma? He feels grateful she's alive, for being a father … He was still a young doctor at the time the photo was taken. He had begun his residency at a small psychiatric unit in Eden Borough, a few miles away from the coast. Eleanor and him had been living in the little coastal town for five years when he bought the Mac Leod's house. As a homebased psychiatrist, he once treated a psychotic historian who told him that the town on the Lothian coast was the miniature copycat of the larger city of Edinburgh. Its resemblance in name was due to the fact that the Scottish suburb had grown along with the sprawling city whose council had wished to reflect in their charter the fact that the little town was built at the foot of a fort. The name "Eden" had been resurrected on the dust of the word Eidyn, a bastard declension of the Brittonic name Gododdin, later superimposed with the Christian name "Eden".

There was always a strange quizzical way, a playful Mona Lisa quietude about that picture of his daughter, he recalls. In her cheeks, he finds his own features; in her chin, her mother's, while in her eyes, there's the wonder of Nature, both him and her, a language only parents understand …

Since Aunt Catherine never missed an opportunity to let him want for more, her account of Charles Dubois' monk-fishing expedition had made his throat dry as he put the phone down. Once the Catherine Hallmark hurricane abated, he had begun fanning the flames of his rusty adventure spirit, a glass of Scotch in hand. Distilling the unsolicited injunctions of his mind, he had weighed his involvement in the quest for the Everblue before inviting Dubois to meet him at his den. The Faustian deal was sealed. He could not deny that he shared the same dishevelled passion for adventure as Aunt Catherine. But she also ignited in him an unabashed sense of hubris and recklessness that he knew would never have materialised without his attraction for Beatrice, her daughter. Bee, who was now staying over more often at his mansion, had complained that her mother was becoming a serious concern. Lately, her aura had waned dramatically:

- 'You won't believe it, Unk! I caught her kissing a young man who came round doing the garden. Meanwhile, Herbert is fleecing her; I am worried she might have dementia,' Beatrice had said, snapping the Jack Hardy from the gable wall.
- 'She hasn't got dementia. I should know, I am a doctor! Her COG is desperately normal,' he had retorted with the good-natured protective tone that he reserved for her, knowing full well that Bee had to contend with the love of a narcissistic mother.

He remembers how he had told her that if the Everblue was anything like the Tibetan poppy, he would have no difficulty believing its radiance could turn a monk into a raving lunatic. "God knows political leaders didn't need the Everblue for that", he still hears his joke ring.

He remembers Beatrice walking towards the French window the next morning, after yet another argument with her mother, as if she was striking a sullen pose to freeze their fateful conversation in his memory:

- 'She knows very well what she's doing, but she would also do anything for you. You know that, don't you?' he had said, in way of some fatherly horseshit.
- 'Would she, though?' Bee had said.
- 'I think she would. She's your mother, you've got to give her that, at least,' he had said, trying to assuage her anger.
- 'But Uncle ... Didn't she prey on you too, in a way?
- What do you mean?
- Oh, please ... Everybody in the family knows you were always her minion. Why do you always take her side? Can't you see she's destroying lives around her?
- How dare you!' had erupted Jonathan, awkwardly indignant.

But Jonathan would finally concede that Catherine had ransacked more than a soul.

- 'I'm an old woman's child, and my mother is a child herself!' Beatrice had said, tapping the Jack Hardy crop nervously against the mantelpiece.
- 'How despondent you are, at your age, already!' he had said, 'You haven't seen anything of the world yet!'

But try as he might reassuring her, he had to admit that even he couldn't fathom his aunt's character. He was already fucking his cousin with his eyes, straddled over the French door, musing at Beatrice's strawberry blond hair sway voluptuously as she sauntered towards the stables, as he consciously carved her curves. He remembers how the idea of an expedition started forming in his mind at that very moment. What would happen in the next months, no one could have foreseen, yet everything had followed from his salacious plans. Beatrice was right. Catherine had always bestowed on her nephew dubious favours, gradually bosoming him into submission, grooming his life into indenture. She had contributed to the purchase of the MacLeod's house against her husband's will for starters. He was aware her overflowing attentions were that of a sexual predator. Had he not sought revenge against Catherine by consciously shaping her daughter into his scapegoat? Had he only realised then …

That night, as he contrived to warm her to his idea of a summer holiday in the land of the Everblue, he realised how much he desired the young woman, his cousin, and how his filial duties after her father's death had to recede before his lust for her youth. He could always try and reassure himself as he has done a million times before—his ego still panting for the redeeming hope that Beatrice is still alive—that it was Catherine's introduction of Dubois that had started it all, but to no avail: the guilt keeps eating away at his days like salt at the rock.

Later on, in the evening, he had felt aroused by her tight-fitting riding leggings and her nonchalant pose against the garden wall. It was already too late, he remembers. So bad his manhood was raptured that, in his fantasy, she was promised to him. Soon, his passion would know no bounds.

The pang of guilt smarting even now, as he reminisces over the days that preceded their departure for Japan, he cries out: 'Where is she now?'

If by a miracle, she managed to escape the terrible ordeal he inflicted upon her, he wishes she would turn up right there and then in the doorframe of his study again:

- 'I only need an excuse to get away. I know you will find something to deliver me from the ogre, I can't take it any longer!' had said Beatrice, her eyes shining with rebellious anger.

Origan

The indefatigable horse never failed to surprise her. Even if Origan's show jumping days were over, the stallion unexpectedly regained his fiery character in his old age. All week, as many times before, she rode out her broiled bitterness at her mother's eccentricity. As for Jonathan, the stables had to be revamped so Beatrice could fully give vent to her passion.

Catherine had wanted a child in her fifties, so that Beatrice was born between a train station and a five-star hotel in Cyprus. She had not meant to give birth on the Middle-Eastern Island of volcanoes and the Greek goddess Aphrodite, but Beatrice was nevertheless born under the wild starry skies of the islands the Cypriot poet Leonidas Malenis described as the "golden-green leaf thrown into the sea".

Since the death of her father, Jonathan had become a de facto surrogate father for Beatrice. But Beatrice soon turned eighteen. Kicking the hornet's nest like her mother was not in her character, although Jonathan could feel the shadow of his aunt bubbling with dark matter under his cousin's alabaster skin. Indeed, she contrasted her mother's exuberance with a stern sobriety that he could feel was beginning to crack at the seams. If she definitely came from the same stock, she had yet to bloom. She called him "Unk", which didn't make things easier for him. Far from emulating her mother's life style, Beatrice had recently contrived a solicitor's PA look, with thick-rimmed adumbrating glasses, as if to better frame her Freudian repression of her mother's loose morals. Her bright green eyes, her blond hair and freckles, her maturing curves and her slightly burked voice tainted with the sweet honey of candidness, were still veiled under the shadows of her mother's stifling narcissism. He would often spy on her in the gash of these two polar identities. But it's how she resembled Eleanor, his late wife, even in the most innocent of idiosyncrasies, that was most uncanny.

He sometimes thought his late wife had been her model —although Beatrice grew up at a distance— and that she had been dipped in the same baths of love.

The fact that she refused to see in herself the extrovert qualities of her matrix made her even more desirable. He suspected that she had fleshed into the object of his fantasy during her early teens, when she began visiting Charles, his monkey. After the death of his wife, Jonathan's heart had revived in her presence. The funeral pyre burning in Eleanor's name turned into the flame of passion around Beatrice's seventeenth birthday before he even construed her as a mature matrix herself. Of course, she would meet a boy, Jake, a twenty-one-year-old autistic lad who studied photography at Eden Borough University. Jonathan remembers how she would be fiercely protective of him. Her voice still rings in the corridors of the Hallmarks' antiquated house of shame:

- 'He's not my boyfriend! He's just a friend, are you jealous?' she would tease him.

As he trolls around the garden in search of a shaded place to sit in the searing summer heat, he remembers how he began feeling aroused by her bashful innuendos. Those were the first signs she was fumbling for a father figure, alone in the darkness of individuation. He had attempted auto-psychoanalysis to dispel his fantasies about her, but without will, there was no way. It had started when he tried to convince himself that her young spirit might still instil some needed vigour into his fatigued soul, that a bit of adventure could help Beatrice spread her wings. He had tried to persuade himself that he was a father, an uncle, the responsible adult, but the predatory cousin lurked behind the broken reeds of grief, crouched and heedful, foaming at the mouth.

- 'I should leave her to her devices. She only sees me when her mood is low! Do you know she speaks ill of Dad, accusing him of making her feel that way, even dead!' he remembers.

Beatrice was crying after yet another argument with her mum. Inside the doorframe leading to the kitchen, she was undecided as to how to deal with the seventy-year-old renegade.

- 'Don't you know your mother by now? And how about you started living your own life, hm? Count your blessings, Bee. You have everything you could possibly wish for, youth, beauty, money,' he had argued.

Beatrice, standing one foot on the sunny mid-evening decking, the other half of her body cast in the shadow of his office, had predictably shirked his compliment:

- 'Beauty? I don't think so.'

He had looked at her incredulous smile tinged with nubile modesty thinking that she could not possibly be unaware of her charms and their effect on his middle-aged ego.

- '"Adversity is the first path to the truth," wrote Byron, he had said cunningly, 'but you still need your mother's wealth!'

She had smiled dubitatively. She must have felt that his remark was overfatherly indeed. But he knew he was only baiting her teenage mania by challenging her rebellious streak, mischievously formalising and reinforcing her anger towards her mother. She was here in his Scottish den because she needed love, and he was all about giving it to her.

- 'I am thinking of a project you might be interested in. It's quite exciting. But it will need some preparation. Has she told you about the Japanese expedition?' he had suggested.

Beatrice had re-appeared fully in the door frame, flustered.

- 'No ... We haven't spoken since Herbert hit on me in the downstairs bathroom!
- What? Oh, Bee, I'm so sorry ... What did your mother have to say about that?
- She ignored me, dismissing the whole thing as a fit of jealousy. She finally apologised, but I know she wants me out of her love nest. The old bitch!
- You know you're always welcome here. I can have a word with her if you want me to,' he had simulated.

But he knew Aunt Catherine wouldn't flinch. He had willy-nilly tried to remind his aunt that the death of Beatrice's father had weakened her daughter's sense of self, but Catherine's attention could not be distracted from her gigolos.

- 'She always was a bit of a selfish peacock,' he conceded that evening, when Beatrice slept over, a bundle of clothes by her bed.
- 'I would do anything! What do you have in mind? What is that Japanese expedition about already?' Bee had asked distractedly.

As he tried to explain to her that a flower in Japan had created a stir, she had looked over at Charles's cage, laughing at the noise he was making, at the bottom of the garden.

- 'Shall we take Charles with us?' she had joked, accepting his offer without even hearing the details.

He had looked at her elegant and slim silhouette as she jumped over a stack of hay towards the stables, relishing the thought of having her to himself for a whole month or even more.

Crying pitifully, even to his standards, he cannot help but break into a ravaging fit of swearing, halting himself, then screaming insanities to God or his own shadow, while relishing the pain inflicted by remembrance in the same breath. He had felt vindicated preying upon her candid soul, taking advantage of her naivety and hunger for any distraction that could put seven seas between her and her mother. It was music to his ears: she wanted a break from Aunt Catherine, and, burnt by his blind desire, he had grabbed the opportunity to string her along in the clasp of his fanciful quest for the damned Everblue.

A Flying Monkey

Charles was born in captivity. He was named after his great-great grandfather, who was a contemporary of Darwin. The name connection with Dubois never sprung to mind until now. They were both called Charles. How strange he had not seen it …

He mechanically takes the garden path to the lab, where Charles, the macaque Rhesus used to welcome him with jittering cries. He became the monkey's guardian after a stint at a pharmaceutical lab, towards the end of his medical residency, before his training as a psychiatrist began. He had salvaged the Rhesus macaque when the pharmaceutical company for which he was doing research discovered a bad kidney gene that plagued the Macaca mulatta specie used for most modern vaccines. Charles had been made redundant …

The barbary ape was the spitting image of his mother, the veteran of the lab, who died when Charles was four. He had the same brown endearing eyes as his mother, the same coarse red skin around the nose, mouth and eyes, and the same tawny fur trimmed with a dark collar; a remnant of the ice age exodus.

Charles' quasi-human expressions made him lose track of time. The macaque never failed to distract him from the dreary routine of psychiatry and the protracted legal expert testimonies that the court always expedited against his best judgment. Still startled by the death of his wife, the monkey had gained his sympathy. Sometimes, by simply looking into his eyes he felt like a child again, as the old-world monkey filled his mind with mischievous thoughts. Charles became his play partner, his friend and confidante. When he watched him jump about the open-air cage, it made him feel care-free, happy again. Sometimes, their inevitable dialogue of the deaf invariably ended up in a cuddle. They would have cognac together, telling each other tall tales, or sharing their feelings about their obdurate solitude.

Charles never reproduced. It felt natural to share those bachelor man-to-monkey moments with a seasoned ration of a twenty-five-year-old scotch, as on that fine day in July, when he took the liberty of toasting the promise of a great adventure, along with Charles' favourite delicacy, quince jelly.

Charles loved his wife too. Jonathan's Eleanor was the most beautiful angel that the sky ever conceived. Without fail, Eleanor infused her organic sense of the world into his clinical mind, so when she passed away in her thirties —he was still a medic, also in his thirties— his whole universe crumbled down. How he had managed to keep his practice open for twenty years after that, he owed it to Charles. To add insult to injury, Jonathan was convinced that he had brought a bad virus home from work when Eleanor became hemophiliac with no previous history. Sometimes, one saw perfectly healthy DNAs yield under some overactive immune response. Of course, there was always a plethora of help at hand in the National Health Service, but sadly, none that was helpful that particular weekend. Eleanor died in hospital from injuries that she suffered in the garden. She had been attending to her rose bush with a secateur in hand and had fallen on the rocky features she proudly spent hours perfecting. He was on call that day. His schedule was punishing. It took hours before someone found her. Once in hospital, her intracranial hemorrhage sadly proved irreversible. Elenaor, his angel, died after a month-long coma. He held her hand and kissed her forehead for the last time before she was pronounced dead by a medical doctor in hospital.

Jonathan dabbles his eyes with his pocket square, a handkerchief that invariably reminds him of his father who had the same habit of having his initials sown on his personal linen: JD, for Jonathan Deadstone and Jerry Deadstone.

As he left the garden of memories that July evening, without knowing why, he could not help peeping into the cage, waiting for Charles to advise him on his next move. But Charles was unusually glum and his counsel would not be much use. Instinctively, he had walked towards the safe vault which the old Scottish Mac Leod patriarch had shown him during his first visit of his future family home. The descendant of one of the Scottish clan chiefs had a gambling addiction and had decided to sell his house fast. His shrink seemed like a good fit. But Jonathan never liked this house. It was Eleanor who had fallen in love with it. A blessing and a curse, Eleanor and her garden irremediably reminded him of her accidental death.

Behind the false door, there was a hidden passage that marked the entrance of the Mac Leod family vault where all manners of cherished and precious collectables were kept during the Scottish clan's tenure. Late to the informal viewing due to a spill-over of patients from one of his colleagues at his Eden

Borough psychiatric cabinet, he had been shown the Chinese vase collection and the fine enamel of the tileworks, as well as the rusty Milners plaque bolted in the secret door, which had filled him with awe. The vault, had said Mac Leod proudly, during his visit, was big enough for one man only.

"Fire resisting" appears from under the dust, as he passes a finger over the rusty iron. But as he marvels at the plaque, where a crown flanked with two bucking horses with flaring manes are engraved, he notices two head-bowed blacksmiths working around a cauldron that he has never seen before. Somehow, this minute detail must have escaped him. He holds on to the enamel handle and pushes the door. The plaque disappears from view as he flings the door open …

How he had found a newspaper advertising "Mein Kampft" to its readers was thanks to the lighting reflected on the secret walled passage that led to a disused office. The first time he broke through the wall, following some vague intuition that a "secret room" was indeed hidden behind the vault's wall, he had found an article in an old newspaper about a sacred flower found in Tibet. Retracing his steps to elucidate the incredible coincidence with Dubois's tale, he had followed the light reflecting on a course of tiles to a hollow sounding square. Taking on the task of dismantling the back wall of the vault to whittle down his dull retirement hours and evade his inseparable grief, he had grasped a sledge hammer and had vented his anger at the wall. It had been a bonding revelation for Beatrice, who had later joined in the fun. They had imagined that they were penetrating the long-buried secrets of some Scottish pharaoh, or maybe a bootlegging hollow or some cloak-and-dagger dugout. He can still see Beatrice's discomfited face at the miserable desk and chair hidden behind the false wall …

The article seen in the Scottish newspaper, before Dubois' visit, next to the Times' "Mein Kampf" publicity, in the secret room behind the MacLeod's vault, must have been playing on his mind after Catherine's call. Dismissing the Nazi vibe as just another crack at the aristocratic British intelligentsia, he had thought the grass was always greener. The quote he had read in one his psychiatric manuals as a student came to mind: "A buddha is as useful as an enemy." "To keep your friend close and your enemy closer" might also have been on his mind, as he imagined the publisher eking out a quick profit before the sobering blitzes. It seemed that humanity had a choice then as always …

The article was so strange in fact, that he had obliterated it all until Catherine's account of her meeting with Dubois. When she mentioned the Everblue on the phone, he was alerted by Charles' playful and noisy games.

Charles had made him think of Catherine, and his blood bond guilt had instinctively pushed him to search the secret place again after her call. Strangely, it seemed that his visit of the MacLeod's vault had managed to scramble his sense of chronological time so that when Dubois visited, he had forgotten all about it …

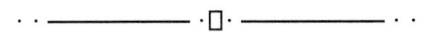

· · ———————— ·◻· ———————— · ·

Esoteric mysteries weren't his forte. Still, he was excited at the thought of hearing the tale from the horse's mouth as it provided the concrete reality needed to hoodwink Beatrice into his grand scheme. Besides, he had not had visitors for a long time. He was also glad that Aunt Catherine wasn't able to make it that night. She would certainly have overreached and he didn't particularly want to interpose himself between his aunt and her daughter.

A few hours before Dubois' arrival, Beatrice took her favourite exercise saddle from the saddle rack and busied herself in the stables while he followed amorously her comings and goings. He listened with a gleeful heart to the clopping of the horse receding as he saw Origan's fierce mane elope under a wet overcast sky. She had had yet another heated argument with her mother on the phone. She was safely under his wing now.

Dubois was expected at 3.30 p.m., but was early. The Frenchman had meant to wander around the countryside beforehand, but a drizzle had started to fall so that he had cut his stroll short. He turned up on his doorstep at 3 p.m., explaining why he abhorred the Scottish rain. His nemesis was a liquid personalisation of everything he hated about the northern weather, with its stark drops in temperature and relentless darkness. Dubois' enthusiastic demeanour made an unforgettable entrance into his life as Jonathan offered him a sake once he finally removed his full-length rain coat and layers of wool. Dampened introductions were made and Dubois said he was feeling a feminine presence in his host's home:

- 'Ah, yes. She's the niece of Mrs. Hallmark, isn't she? Yes, I met her quickly at your aunt's mansion,' Dubois said, amused.
- 'Would you care for a Japanese pick-me-up, Mr. Dubois?'
- Oh, yes please.'

They sat in his study. A storm broke out and they chatted about the weather over sharp tearing roars of thunder. Dubois joked that the storm sounded like someone was breaking furniture in a giant echo chamber. Charles said that he felt "drilled" by his professional stare:

- 'Oh, don't worry. I don't usually offer sake to my patients,' Jonathan reassured him.
- 'Somehow, spirits tell us a lot about their country of origin,' Dubois remarked, 'They speak a language that only seasoned drinkers understand. Mouth and sensory organs are mere go-betweens, don't you think? They enable the communication between the wild world of craft and the distilled magic of natural essences,' Dubois was pompously arguing, contemplating the glass and its content, as if he was admiring a precious stone.
- 'And the feeling is only complete when all parts of the body have relinquished their dependency on the mind,' Jonathan joked expertly.
- 'I must say I have not been that much entertained in a long time. Your aunt Catherine is quite the character. Thoroughly pleased to meet you all nevertheless. She's told me a lot of good about her nephew, the doctor, or the "shrink" as she says, not the least is your passion for plants, I believe? I am thoroughly excited to get to know you all,' said Dubois.

The holistic bliss of that well-crafted beverage would have been wasted on the old dowager, had argued Jonathan, who joked openly at the expense of his aunt. A charming man that Dubois, he had thought, despite his initial rant at the Scotissh weather. He spoke perfect English, so annoyingly so that his thick-cut French accent felt like a consolation.

- 'I understand perfectly that no one wants a spy from across the Channel mooching around their mansion,' Dubois joked.

Catherine had insisted Dubois should be flanked by a chaperone on his first and last visit of the estate; incidentally, one of Catherine's handy staff.

- 'You could easily be mistaken for one,' Jonathan said, handing him another cup of sake.

Dubois had laughed at Jonathan's wisecrack about his long trenchcoat and hat. They jeered at the old sod all evening. The moiré green sofa facing the large bookcase full of early Victorian travel books and antique manuscripts had occupied their first hour of conversation. Dubois had a mystifying smile and a mocking demeanour about him that had taken like a spark to his dry fire starter. He was of stocky built but had an effeminate quality about his face that seemed to have stood the test of time. Under his placid exterior, a brilliant mind was evidently bubbling with energy. One detail had stricken Jonathan as he listened to Dubois describing his love for his native countryside. Apart from his expressive eyes, his facial expressions were nearly imperceptible, as if his face was cast in plastic.

Jonathan had invited him to stay over in case the storm worsened. The Frenchman, thankful for Deadstone's invitation, had carried on describing his expedition in detail. He thought the Japanese people were curt. He seemed embittered by their treatment of his person, as if, behind their legendary vicariousness, he had deplored, an ominous backstabbing revengefulness was lurking.

- 'Surely, not all Japanese people are like that guide who visibly didn't like you,' Jonathan argued in defence of the sake.
- 'I know, I shouldn't generalize, but as an anthropologist, I can tell you that there is a quiet suspicion about white foreigners that is not entirely imputable to Hiroshima. They are generally dismissive of our input. I think you might call it 'gaslighting'. It's quite understandable, because of the atrocious consequences of a nuclear bomb, but there is more … There is an inborn cruelty. Some savage and animistic energy. Besides, I wonder if our expedition was totally understood.
- Ah! The Sacred Mountain,' Jonathan said, concerned that the mood had to be swayed swiftly towards the business at hand, since the real prize of the evening, Beatrice, would come back imminently from her ride.

Jonathan had surprised himself saying:

- 'Don't they know that what is sacred is also to be shared?'
- Indeed, what is sacred must remain so, and for it to remain so, it has to be shared, otherwise no one would know it is indeed sacred. And since I could see my polite reminders didn't hit the mark, I became totally antipathetic towards my guide, and finally dismissed him for good.
- Did you find a replacement?' asked Jonathan.
- 'No, but by then, I knew the area quite well. And I felt truly vindicated when I approached the monk on my own. I can speak a bit of Japanese, you see. With the guide looking over my shoulders, I would never have heard of the flower or met Master Khul.'

Jonathan quizzed him at length about his travels that night. His most notable study had been the Inuits and the Thule, in Western Alaska. Dubois was convinced there were the same tribes that had settled in China and Japan five to ten thousand years ago.

- 'Tell me Charles, what is your take on the monk's sudden madness?
- How do you mean "madness"?'

"Damned Catherine and her exagerrations," thought Jonathan.

- 'I mean, why do think the monk went off trail?'

Dubois had looked at him quizzically, as if he doubted the pertinence of his question.

- 'The quarrel with the guide meant that I travelled alone for weeks, wandering between the temples, the forest and the mountains. I found the monk bathing and then, stayed with him in a little shack that recluse Japanese communities had inhabited in the 70s,' said Dubois.

From his elegant leather satchel, Dubois had produced some pictures of the interior of those dilapidated dwellings which the monk and himself had resolved to haunt for the best part of the summer. In the abandoned lodgings, they were strange objects from a bygone age: personal items, such as shoes or kettles, photos of moustached Japanese men in their shrank woolies and flaring pants, a telephone without dial, a jaded chinked tea set, and women in aprons posing on sepia photos. None of them smiling. Everything indicated that the inhabitants had left in a hurry ...

- 'The fear of the atomic bomb must have pushed these town dwellers towards the mountains,' Jonathan said authoritatively.
- 'But what made them leave is a mystery,' said Dubois, 'To cut a long story short, the monk told me about his residency at the temple, as well as his induction aged twenty-one, his murky past before his life among the spartan monks, the routine of his prayers and meditations; that is, until his seniors ostracised him.

Jonathan had let his mind wander as if he was discovering the abandoned village himself, moving from one room to another in dilapidated branch-strewn shacks frozen in time, and whose preserved interiors abounded with relics of a fragile humane presence.

- 'I lost sight of the monk when the weather turned to heavy downpours in near freezing temperatures, in September,' Dubois added, 'The harsh weather is probably the reason why inhabitants finally sought creature's comforts in town, in the 1980's, when things got back to normal. Autumns can be harsh in the north of Japan.
- Wait ... How did you lose sight of him?' Jonathan wondered.
- 'I spent a few days with the monk, as I said. He had become a cast-out since his hierarchy had forced him to ramble aimlessly. He must have felt like a sudden rush to decamp. I couldn't say how he ended up there, as the monastery was miles away, but then he disappeared on me!
- What? Because he wandered up a path that had been condemned? Was that the reason why he had been ostracised?' Jonathan asked, rooting for the defrocked monk.
- 'My point exactly. How spurious that a monk should be blamed for discovering an illuminating path and the most entrancing flower that ever grew on the planet. It simply didn't make sense. You see what I

mean, don't you? But let me tell you how he disappeared,' said Dubois, still visibly aggrieved.

Jonathan had suggested that the monk's actions might have brought discredit on his superiors, which would have loosely warranted his demotion.

- 'Yes, I can see how his hierarchy might have found his behaviour somewhat disqualifying but I doubt this was the whole story,' Dubois remarked penetratingly.

He could make out the anthropologist's method more clearly now under the green art deco stained glass lamp shade. How his body, the living proof of his experience, remembered his companion. The psychiatrist felt that Dubois had been harrowed after the disappearance of the monk, towards whom he had felt a powerful spiritual and natural bond. But, as his speech became more excited, less mentally controlled, his French accent also became more pronounced and his grammar looser. Dubois, who was obviously enjoying the sake, was speaking jubilantly about his experience:

- 'Yes, he should have known better! And, just like you, I was sure he hadn't been ostracised for the reason he gave. I imagine that, seeing how the flower changed his mind about the validity of his religious beliefs, this new world of fantasy probably made him realise he was better off alone to embark on some alternative spiritual journey. I can only testify to the monk's tongue wagging wildly during his trances. I also witnessed something strange … As we spent several days in the abandoned village, among the memorabilia left behind, among that sentimental past that people had rather not face any more, objects appeared and disappeared. It wasn't the first time such ghost villages popped up in the forest in fact. So that, before long, I feared that our village might have just been an illusion,' said Dubois.

Jonathan had pricked his ears …

- 'Something to do with the fact that there may have been a brutal death or something similar, maybe some ritualistic revelation. It remains that the flower was part of it all. The monk's description left me in no doubt that the flower was venerated by those people of the Hiroshima generation who had been scarred by nuclear radiation. Their spirit could have been crystallized in that flower. They are animistic people after all.'

Jonathan was agreeable to the theory that if one focussed long enough on an object or any living thing, it could become a fixation and acquire magical properties.

- 'According to the monk, it wasn't in aloof temples that knowledge was to be found, but among those outcasts inhabiting a lost paradise. The villagers might have infused their lives with the flower and vice versa. It's as if their parallel world had been preserved in timelessness. I didn't know the whole truth about what kind of life the monk might have lived before. I don't know, because he vanished the night I meant to ask him, but it seemed to me that he was a bit too secretive about his days prior to his monkhood,' said Dubois.
- 'So, he vanished from the ghost village in the end?' asked Jonathan.

Dubois was now red in the face because of the roaring fire and sake.

- 'I know it sounds crazy. But it wasn't the first time he had gone into a trance and disappeared before my eyes. Suddenly, like that, pfiut! He would reappear a few minutes later, but outside, in the darkness of the night, in some other place. One night, I was left gaping, trembling with anticipation in one of the shacks, spying on his silhouette that I could barely recognise in the moonlight. One minute he was here and the next, gone! Bemused and terrified, I was. It was quite disturbing! When I asked him about the how and why, he couldn't say or didn't seem to find it extraordinary that he had disappeared. Besides, during his trances, he rambled in a dialect that I didn't know. Even when recorded, once played to the locals, it didn't match any language they knew. It was all Greek to them, except for a song that he sang, which some locals identified as an old tune from the Eido period. And one night, he but all vanished for good. I had barely had time to get used to those sordid disappearances! By then, I was ready to accept these magical happenings as part of a dreamlike state that we shared. It wasn't the first time I would have been given a hallucinogenic drug by tribes I was studying. We had come upon a stack of loose tea left behind by the previous inhabitants, which was incredibly preserved but also of dubious origins!

- I wouldn't be surprised if you had been drinking aspergillus or some kind of ergot, Charles. I did suspect it might have been the tea … My bearings in the ghost village, as you can imagine, were hazy at best. I was seriously beginning to lose my mind. I searched all through the night but couldn't find any trace of him. The next day, a set of tea cups and a tea pot—may I say, completely new—, were left by my bedside. Well, I already knew that there was more than met the eye with this monk, but I also wanted to find that flower. I just needed the guts to hang around, but I didn't, and that's why I am going back there as soon as I can, but with a stronger team, this time,' said Dubois, resolute.

Jonathan thought that since that flower had such an exceptional spiritual significance, why did Dubois not keep the matter secret? He shared his concern with him:

- 'May I give you a gentle warning about this, Charles … In my opinion, and I'm sure you'll agree, as soon as the world knows about the magic flower, you're likely to see a pack of hyenas turn the whole bloody mountain into a tourist attraction!'

Charles nodded gravely:

- 'I get what you're saying … I haven't finalised the details yet, but I can promise you there will be a handful of us on that mountain and you will be the first to know about it.'

Dreamcast

The blue lotus, the sacred narcotic lily of the Nile, floated in his pond, at the height of summer. It was then that his plans to take part in the Everblue expedition crystallised. Since January, his intense relationship with Beatrice had reached a climax of suppression that had him slowly edge towards madness. His curvaceous cousin was haunting his dreams, her face sometimes replacing that of Eleanor in his delirium. During his most loosened drug-induced wanderings, they would have an immaterial baby, a metaphysical child that acquired a physical presence in his empty house. Even during his waking hours, he would sometimes see the imaginary child roaming around the furniture, frolicking about his newly-fangled home.

His appointment with the oncologist was at noon. He had been diagnosed with a leukemia several months before and the consultant had written to him with an update. During that particularly scorching summer, when he reached the clinic, he found the heat in the waiting room intolerable. No air conditioning had been installed and by orders of the Ministry of Health, windows had to stay closed due to the Covid pandemic that had just broken out. Jonathan felt he was lucky that the clinic should still be open. Lately, even GPs had shut their surgery in a hallucinating move that would only have been possible in the worst dystopian nightmare. His name flashed on the electronic display. Dr. Azimov opened the door:

- 'The waiting room is an oven, you could fry an egg!' Jonathan said, chirpy but extremely tired.
- 'Or a steak of salmon,' Azimov said. 'Sorry, dead-pan humour.'

Jonathan sat down, feeling an ominous sense of doom, as Azimov looked suspiciously at his computer screen.

- 'I trust you have my results, doctor?

- Sure.
- And?
- I will go straight to the point, Dr Deadstone, it's not good.
- I'm no stranger to my body's ups and downs, but I guess I needed confirmation.
- It's now stage three, I'm afraid,' Azimov said gravely.

Jonathan had readied himself for the news, but you can never be ready to hear that you're going to die at forty-six. As he ate a sandwich on a bench opposite the Eden Borough clinic, in the small town he had lived all his married life, he wondered how many had sat there, pondering their diagnostic. He realised there and then that the Everblue had just made it to the top of his bucket list. If what Aunt Catherine had said was true, the Everblue could change his destiny. He had to be part of that, at least.

Once home, he tried the narcotic flower on himself. He would note down his motivations for his experiment, even if his conscious use of the flower as an offering, a funeral pyre for his brain, didn't need to be explained. Just before his early retirement, he had used it on his patients. After all, it was his unconscious attraction and violent desire for Beatrice that he had meant to disentangle. Stupidly, he had thought that, to heal his affliction, he needed to become the shaman of her soul, with a vague justification that that soul needed purifying. It was all bound to crash and yet, he couldn't bear the thought of not guiding her to that sacred place.

He decided that a single bud of the sleeping draught would suffice. It's the fresco of Akhenaton, dating from the 14th century BC, that had given him the idea. He had seen it in the Staatliche museum, in Berlin. The fresco represented a deity offering mandrakes and a bud of the blue water lily to an invalid. The scene had made such an impression on his mind that he had decided to plant mandrakes in his own garden and water lilies in his pond. The mandrake roots had died, but the water lily had flourished. After all, during his hypnosis sessions, mandrake, water lily and opium poppies were ingredients that he had used on the travellers of the sacred journey of the spirit in order to induce transcendental visions. He had induced hypnosis on his patients using his home-made potion on many occasions, with sometimes unexpected but probant results.

Wasn't it the case that Tutankhamen's golden tomb had been robbed of the sealed vessels containing the "didi", the potent hypnotic, in preference to the gold? Why would robbers disregard the precious loot for the potions, had he argued in a medical journal, if it wasn't indeed sacred? He had dismissed the eternal life claim of the Egyptian lore, but had worked tirelessly to combine the opioids and narcotics in his lab. All he had to do now was to try the potion on himself …Now, water lilies are a special vessel for the spirit. The trance-inducing narcotic helped pharaohs ease their passage in the after-world. *What better way to go*, he had thought, as he contemplated the poised lily lulling over the pond. Looking back, it's probably his death wish that fed his lurid lust for Beatrice. All the more reason to investigate.

In the cult of Osiris, according to which Egyptian priests gathered in devotion to the prehistoric Egyptian God, rituals performed with the water lily were meant to reenact the birth of the first human being. According to those legends, the first being had been said to arose from the blue water lily. The flower only bloomed for three consecutive days, opening at eight o'clock in the morning, under the middle-eastern sun, to close at the sun's apex. In his Scottish garden, the flower had but a couple of hours of life in the full sun of the summer solstice. It rose on its stem to eight inches over the surface of the pond at noon, when he cut it using Eleanor's secateurs.

Comfortably sat in his study armchair, Jonathan took a thimble of brandy and swallowed the flower. Psychodysleptic effects were immediate, and a trance-like tsunami overtook him before he could press the video recording button …

In his stupor, he saw Osiris' head talking to his physical self, but instead of being adorned with the uraeus, the symbolic Cobra, the head of the Egyptian God was coiffed with a snake-like stem of mandrake bearing a water lily bud while hieroglyphs tangibly sprouted out of his mouth, pouring into Jonathan's open soul, as he felt washed up in his own body. Under the influence of the narcotic power of the flower, Jonathan felt submerged with the awe of motherhood, giving birth to himself. Feeling hollow at first, he gradually felt invested with Osiris' after-life spirit as he saw the snake-like stem turning inwards, boring with cosmic energy into the layers of his consciousness. He then felt the resins of the flowers being poured down over his head so that his body seemed to be cast into a pleasant tetany of warmth, but a deceptive illusion of eternity soon followed.

Meanwhile, his spirit was held aloft to see it all unfold: the ascension towards the plateau, the death of Dubois, the last push towards the summit and the bountiful death brought forth by the ephemeral flower.

Until his body began to spasm. Nerves and muscles, strained like metallic cables, pulling his center away in multiple directions, he tried to resist at first, but the sensation of his body being quartered suddenly condensed in his chest, where a tingling feeling alerted his senses. Trapped in his ephemeral sarcophagus, he saw a gleaming sword, bodies falling under the blade, blood running off down crevices, flesh and bones spluttering on stones, and finally, a decapitated head, rolling down the frozen ground of a cave. Jonathan's alter ego, the Egyptian God, was being murdered in front of his eyes …He opened his eyes in emergency, feeling both conflicted and bruised, his rib cage hurting atrociously. Collecting his thoughts in the middle of the room, looking at the stem of the blue lily flower dangling at the surface of the pond, he realised that he had just been the witness of things to be. It was a precognition of the Everblue expedition's last moments.

But a shameful feeling suddenly overtook him amidst his after-trance state. If he knew that the expedition would end that way, and that he did not stop it, was he not responsible for Beatrice's disappearance?

Long Live Charles

His bluish hand laid limp over the sofa's armrest. The same moiré green that she knew to be his favourite snug had a familiar worn varnish to it. For a moment of incontrollable inertia, she thought of the exoskeletons that were displayed in the study cabinet. She looked again at the haloed hand in the shining morning light seeping through the thick brown curtains, usually drawn during the day. Gaping at the discoloured flesh, she understood straight away what had happened. She gasped, crying with melancholy.

'His favourite couch was where he wanted to die,' she murmured inaudibly.

The nostalgic observer of a lifeless body usually cringes with a feeling of fear mixed with disgust. It is a universal revulsion that needs no subtitles. But seeing his hairy arm behind the cushions as she moved closer, she felt a sense of relief. She loved him so very much.

She attributed this sordid end to last week's excitement about the expedition and the meetings with Dubois, which had intensified as the possibility of an expedition was scaffolded with frantic enthusiasm. It was too much for his heart. The excited over affective bites, the raucous cries, the blood pressure spikes had all but conjugated to this prodigious terror.

Charles passed away peacefully in his home, at Dr. Jonathan Deadstone's mansion, in the early hours of July, 14th. She found him sprawled on the velvet sofa, as if he had taken his ultimate nap and forgot to wake up. The monkey was no more. She heard a tune sifting from the music room. Peeped in to see her uncle playing a jazzy melody that he was obviously improvising. She felt suddenly out of sorts, as if three were a crowd, so that she tiptoed towards the front door and left.

The next morning, Beatrice tried to call Dubois. Her uncle had been apathetic for a few days, refusing to dispose of the body. She felt as if she had to do something about his protracted state, but didn't quite know what. His heavy heart was tramelled by a shadowy halo she could not shake him from, even with the coolest songs on her phone: "I'll be there for you, no matter where you are …"

Later, in her room, at her mother's house, Beatrice listened to the singer's heart-wrenching inflexions. She knew the song and the rap part was expected any second, but she couldn't remember if it came before or after the second chorus; her mind was too busy texting Jake about Charles' passing as Dubois was unavailable:

- 'So, sad!
- Yep' (crying emoticon)
- 'You coming to my Unk's?
- Not sure, need cheddar.
- YOLO, right?
- Ok, then.'

Suddenly, her phone rang:

- 'Dr Deadstone, is he okay?' Dubois enquired, with an empathetic voice.
- 'He's sullen, as you can imagine. They used to have cognac together. I mean … It says it all!
- Yes, I know what you mean. What a shame,' sighed Dubois. 'I wish I could do something, but do please let him know, a week on Wednesday, we will meet with a few potential parties. I have some good news that will cheer him up. We are going to Tomurauchi, do or die! Despite the circumstances of course …I understand, will let him know. I will be there,' said Bee.
- 'Are you coming too?' said Dubois.
- 'Yes, is that a problem?
- Well, of course not, we need young blood, I mean, the world needs young people like you. Will see you on Wednesday,' said Dubois.
- 'Goodbye, Charles.'
- 'Goodbye, Beatrice.'

Beatrice didn't make it in time to the meeting with Dubois. Instead, in the afternoon, while the symposium of eminent flower hunters was taking place, she opened the front door of her mother's bedroom to find two men, one of whom very young, prostrated before Catherine's abandoned body, sprawled out like a diva singing her most popular chorus on a matinée in the West End. Beatrice gawped at the bed scene for a few seconds until their eyes crossed. A mischievous smile on her mother's face made her turn around in shock and disgust as she heard her extravagant wailing:

- 'It was completely impromptu, my dear, oh, come on!' said Catherine Hallmark.

Light-headed, her waist leaning on to the balustrade mid-flight, Beatrice heard Catherine's laugh ricochet. As it seemed unlikely the picture of the fawning matrix would ever be erased from her memory, she ran towards the driveway. Infuriated, she swore she would never step foot in her mother's house again. The moral high ground of teenage angst crippling her pride, she felt like the world was eating her alive as she got into the mini cooper. Angry and sad at her mother's desecration of her father's memory, revolted and subserviently magnanimous, she felt like puking at the wheel all over the world of adulthood. But a sense of freedom began overriding her conflicted feelings. Erupting in her seventy-year-old mother's bedroom while she was having sex with two young men was the dramatic moment she had been waiting for to give herself a head start. She drove to the haven she knew was waiting for her and found her uncle waiting with open arms …

Conspiracy

Jake Edwards-Angst was twenty-one, three years older than Beatrice, so that the idea of being introduced to him made Jonathan sick to his stomach. He was certain that his cousin had decided off her own bat that her new boyfriend would accompany them to the sacred mountain. Without even asking for his blessing, she had imposed the young man's stub and pimples into their ethereal tent.

- 'Did I tell you that this house belonged to the MacLeòids of Lewis?' said Beatrice, guiding Jake's first steps inside her uncle's castle.
- 'I am beginning to think that you might resemble your mother more than I had imagined,' Jonathan said abruptly, turning away from them both, shuffling directionless.
- 'I beg your pardon?' said Beatrice.

She apologised to Jake and marshalled her uncle by the arm to the kitchen.

- 'Are you for real? Would you mind telling me what this shitshow is all about?' said Beatrice.
- 'I am sorry … I spoke out of turn. I don't know what I meant to say, but it came out the wrong way. I would have liked a heads up before meeting with your new boyfriend, that's all. Did you tell him about our plans?' said Jonathan, suddenly passible.

Beatrice stood back against the closed kitchen pine door. She did not see his crumpled constricted face, looking down at the Terracotta tiles. Now, his vindicative grin infuriated her.

- 'He's not my boyfriend! He's just a friend, are you seriously jealous?'

She now stared at him, peering down the depth of incomprehension that had materialised between them.

- 'No. Of course not! What, jealous of a pot-head? I am entitled to know who you date, aren't I?' said Jonathan, rubbernecking her remark, hoping to catch her eyes with his confused and atoning pug impersonation.

Her finger wagging in the air, she now looked at him straight in the eye, like a mother scalding her child.

- 'I can't believe it. You *are* jealous! And what makes you think he's a pothead?' she muttered in exasperation. 'Jake is autistic by the way, so whatever you say, it won't land the way you think. He must feel so uncomfortable, right now. Seriously!'

He then walked towards her, held her gently by the small of her back, and in an attempt to calm her down, suddenly smooth and jazzy suave said:

- 'Bee, do you remember when you cried in my arms after your father died? Was I jealous, then? I am protecting you, that's all! And it's true, I am a bit annoyed at your *faux-pas*. But let's forget about it. I'll be careful with Jake. You've just confirmed my suspicions about his autism. How did it go with Origan this morning?' said Jonathan, now mellowed.
- 'He was a bit snaky, I think he needs a mare, like you,' said Beatrice.

She turned on her heels, jolted the door and walked back to the lobby where Jonathan followed her, his tail between his legs. Jake was looking dull-eyedly at the picture of staghorm moss displayed on the wall. Jonathan couldn't help but size him up when Beatrice noticed suitcases in the hallway:

- 'What were you planning to do, Uncle?
- I wish you'd stop calling me uncle. Technically, I'm your cousin.
- O … kay, and where were you planning to get to with those suitcases, Unk?

- I was merely rehearsing,' said Jonathan.
- 'What, you timed packing up your suitcases and running up and down the stairs, did you?' said Beatrice.

Jake and Beatrice chortled in unison before she finished introducing them. Jake was a photographer. They met at the Student hall.

- 'Glad to meet you Jake. Now, I simply wasn't told you were coming, but if you care for a pauper's dinner, be my guest. Breakfast like a king, lunch like a lord and, dine like a pauper, well. That's my motto!' said Jonathan, mundanely.

His ego felt suddenly sullen and bruised as their laughs rang like an unwanted jingle in his head. This incursion smarted the place in his heart where an innocent Beatrice lived. Charles might have left a void that was difficult to fill, but his behaviour didn't need to be so blatantly obvious. He could at least have tried and disguised his heady jealousy. But he wouldn't be swayed by Jake's so-called get-out-free-card autism. He was decided to stake him out for any signs of physical attraction towards Beatrice. Still, it was too early to contemplate going on this expedition on his own even if he felt hurt by her derisive tone. The sight of her new friend called him back to reason. Reality had made a sudden irruption into his esoteric world. His ears drawn back, his back rounded, his hairs raised at the sight of the complicit nubile freedom they shared around the table, Jonathan felt his martyr pelt shrink uncomfortably. He weighed telling Beatrice about his cancer, and finally held back the admission in confidence. He would tell her as a last resort, if every else but pity got him her good graces.

As he sensed their energetic teenage auras mingling, fearing that anything could spring at any moment between the two of them, Jonathan struggled to rein in his covetous streak, bent on tanking their animated diner conversation as best as he could.

- 'You look tired, Unk. Jake and I will sort ourselves out, don't worry. You don't have to stay up with us,' said Beatrice sharply.

He felt Jake's smile as deprecatory, as if he had already seen through Jonathan's infatuation for Beatrice underneath his show of protective love.

Jonathan felt like an outcast, staring into the jungle of nubile complicity, but was determined to stake his claim. He stalled the young people's dynamics by drilling Jake about his studies, hoping to make him pass for a teenage clod.

- 'I'll fulfil my duty as a host, if you don't mind, Bee,' said Jonathan.

Beatrice suddenly realised Jonathan was feeling genuinely alienated. A few days had passed since the crowd of voracious adventurers had gathered around Dubois's project. Now, she pitied him. His cheese and biscuits diner must have suddenly felt too pickled, so that she pressed him for his account of the meeting:

- 'Right. We were at the Emigration Inn, the shady pub on Cross Street, in Eden borough, you and I have been there several times. This is how it went down,' said Jonathan, pleased to be her centre of attention again.

He related the shady pub meal and described the guests attending at Dubois's behest. Two men had been invited. Jonathan had warned Dubois about venting out the secret flower's hypnotic powers and he had felt trumped. Evidently, Dubois had not listened, commented Jonathan. He described three men plotting like kids bent over a dead bird, discussing the best options. One of them belonged to the Institute of Psychospiritual Synthesis, a sectarian theosophical club ran by London aristocrats who were enamoured with Buddhist esoterism. Another guest of Dubois', a trinity College envoy, Director of research Jim Walden, had a neat goatee and a pale complexion that betrayed a sly and cupid scheming streak. The third witch was Walden's secretary, a rotund woman whose name he couldn't remember.

Jake and Beatrice listened. Jonathan was controlling his breathing, feeding their trepident effervescence with mysterious details about the participants. While Jim Walden, of the Trinity College, and his assistant were playing good cop, bad cop, Jonathan explained that it was obvious that they didn't intend to finance the expedition unless they could find a way to wrap themselves in glory about the discovery of the Everblue. The bibulous psychospiritual guru, who was knocking down glasses of sherry as if there were no tomorrow, was wearing sandals, described Jonathan, as the nincompoop psychologized on the discovery and its importance for the evolution of the mind. He was mincing his words as if they were boluses of gold. Jonathan had recorded the whole meeting on his mobile, so played it to them so they could hear Doherty's voice, as the preposterous guru harped on his credentials as a transcendental psychologist. They laughed. Jonathan was pleased he had won them over with his jokes at the expense of Doherty. He then explained how he had felt a chill down his spine, at Dubois's duplicity. He thought he had heard him say that the expedition was an entombed secret. Nevertheless, counting on the Trinity College to waste time in branding the expedition with their purple shield and Royal standard, Beatrice and him were left with some time to organise themselves, albeit still expectant on Dubois, the guardian of the Everblue's secret location. These details seemed to answer Beatrice's question about the suitcases in the hall:

- 'This Charles Dubois came round to your house, didn't he?' mulled Beatrice.
- 'Yes, he came while you were riding. But he promised me he would be diligent.
- Do you think he has already set eyes on the flower?
- I don't think he has.
- Then, we must go pronto! Beat them to the post, Unk!' said Beatrice.
- 'Except, I don't know where the flower is,' said Jonathan, mortified.

At least, Beatrice was still on board. Jonathan felt synchronised with her again. While the Trinity College was finessing the details of their colonising entreprise, Beatrice and him would make some headway. Dubois and the psychospiritual guru would be part of the expedition. But he wasn't ready to tell Beatrice and her pet about the possible deleterious regressive effect of the flower just yet. It would have complicated everything. Besides, had Dubois even seen the flower? If he had, why wasn't he raving mad like the monk? Was the monk even raving mad? There were too many questions left unanswered. It was best Beatrice didn't know. Meanwhile, Jonathan's character assessment had confirmed his intuitions. During his medical career, he hadn't never seen a man so cunning as to avoid his diagnostic. He had seen his fair share of lunatics, including in the prison system, but no one ever fooled him. Not once. Dubois was no more mad than Jake was autistic …While Beatrice shared her excitement about going to Japan with Jake, he couldn't help but try and gauge the young man's introvert negativism as he began describing his doomed vision and his photographic ambitions. Beatrice, Jonathan noticed, couldn't stop nurturing his ego with endearing small ear-whispering teasers to which Jake smiled halfwittedly. Jake then told them about his job as liner for the local press. As he drilled Jake about his origins, amidst the medieval décor of his Scottish mansion, it became obvious to Beatrice that her uncle was putting her friend through a character assessment. Between two glasses of wine, Beatrice noticeably glanced at him and rolled her eyes, trying to steer the conversation towards the wordly matter of climate change to find a common ground:

- 'Soon, you'll see private jets with plutocrats on board hopping from one summit to another while the rest of us drown under tsunamis and biblical deluge,' said Jake in the way of an olive branch.
- 'Does that mean that you wish to photograph the end of world?' asked Jonathan, rolling the sour wine of jealousy around his tongue.
- 'No, I just love Nature as a subject,' said Jake 'Once, for instance, I was sitting in a deserted public park. It must have been one of those twilight moments when you rarely find yourself in a public place on your own. You see what I am saying? Suddenly, I heard like a noise and noticed it came from the tree behind me, right?
- Creepy!' said Beatrice, as if magic was pouring out of his lips.
- 'Trees were ejaculating their seeds down below. It was September. A horse chestnut's conkers were falling all around the tree bole,' said Jake.

Beatrice beamed at Jake's metaphor.

- 'Wow, it must have been freaky, right?' she said, inebriated by the wine, egging Jake on, while keeping an eye on her uncle's reactions.
- 'It's just nature!' said Jonathan, toning down their excitement.
- 'Men hate trees, you know. They are dwarfed by them, all of them are. No exception. That's why they cut them down without mercy,' continued Jake.
- 'Greed is the reason why!' fuelled Beatrice, siding with Jake.
  'It's not just about money or landgrab, it's pure hatred,' she said.
- 'I didn't know you'd started a cult?' Jonathan said jokingly to Beatrice, who, nettled, darted her frowning green eyes at him.
- 'Aye, hubris is the killer of good will,' said Jake, sheepishly.
- 'Do carry on, Jake … ' Beatrice spurred him on, enthusiastically.

- 'Then, I heard a music box playing its lullaby. It was coming from a bin, like ghosts playing among the living.
- Good lad! You couldn't find a better metaphor for what the planet needs, another Gothic revival,' said Jonathan. Beatrice looked at Jonathan reproachfully.
- We procrastinate, declaring war here and there to pass the time, while self-concerned despots divide and conquer the world to find new revenue streams. But the real issue gets swept under the carpet of ignorance.
- Blimey, wee lad!' Jonathan said to their surprise, 'And what is it that they are ignorant about?
- Well, obviously, the less trees you have the less oxygen you breathe, and the more CO_2 is in the atmosphere. What's so difficult to understand?' said Jake, placidly shrugging his shoulders.

Jonathan gawped at his prudential cheese and biscuits, pondering the distance he felt had grown between his feelings for Beatrice and his reasonable self. He left them to their excited discussion at the table to smoke a cigar in the lobby. He found himself gawking at a stained-glass door picturing a fishing scene under a yellow glass chandelier and an art deco sun well. The door was still shaking on its hinges. He realised he had taken his frustration out on the door by pushing it violently. In the next room, he gazed at the carved wood roses of the fire surround, and its elaborate gothic stone relief. Looking directly towards the panoramic recessed alcove looking onto the garden, he gazed at the subdued Scottish daylight seeping in listlessly. It had been Eleanor's favourite room. It was now an empty mausoleum ... "This was you seeping through the window," he said to himself, standing in the same room, as if the dust accumulated over the past months had barely coated his dulled memories of the dinner. His punishment for his delusion were those painfully vivid memories of love lost, and avid feelings he had selfishly projected on to Beatrice, his cousin and protégé. He was watching his own living light waning, as the rumour of the dinner resurfaced in his mind. It was that night that Beatrice's fate was decided. He knows the taste of those tears, but the trail of his thoughts relentlessly brings him back to the same night. Once the meal was over, he showed Jake his library, out of courtesy for Beatrice:

- 'A thesaurus of Jurassic proportions, Mr. Deadstone,' said Jake, wittingly.
- 'What's that? Oh, I love plants, you see. That's why those books are all about botany and plants!' he said.
- 'I see you have exoskeletons, do you study beetles too, Mr. Deadstone?'

Jake fumbled in his pockets for something he wanted to show Jonathan.

- 'Yes, I do. I also had a monkey, but he's dead now. He used to keep me company, you know,' said Jonathan.
- 'I have found this golden scarab on the dark web,' Jake said with pride.
- 'May I see it?'
- 'Sure.
- It would appear I have seen this somewhere, but can't remember where exactly. Is it a talisman of some sort?'
- 'I don't know,' said Jake, disconcerted.
- 'Google it, you'll find ancient Egyptian cults would see that as a symbol of resurrection, a sign from the after-life. The exoskeleton of insects is the envelope that dies. For humans, the true envelope lies within. Jung, the psychiatrist and visionary, invented the concept of synchronicity listening to a patient who saw one just like this in his dreams, when suddenly during their therapy session together, a beetle landed on Jung's cabinet window sill. Both were puzzled, I imagine.
- Wow, "synchronicity" is what happens to me all the time,' said Jake.

Dubiously magnanimous, he showed Jake a volume on mushrooms, pretending to enjoy imparting some fatherly knowledge onto his younger guest. He had meant to slowly inch the cautionary statement about Beatrice at the first opportunity. He should have been kinder to Jake whose selfless acts on the mountain would later save his life. Instead, he had been antipathetic to him, spending the best of the evening trying to nip their friendship in the bud. In retrospect, his plan to push Jake away was gratuitously callow. Using the topic of mushrooms as a pretext to tell him to back off Beatrice was even more ludicrous.

- 'I love that picture on your wall, Jonathan. What is it?' said Jake.

- 'It's Amanita muscaria, a toxic mushroom'
- 'And where is that place?'
- 'I bought the print in Cornwall. Eleanor, my late wife and I had the most delicious times there. It's Mevagissey, I have some very dear friends there, you know … Actually, I was told recently about an abandoned village in Japan where the inhabitants left a wad of exciting memorabilia. It would make a great footage, I am sure. It seems that a photographer would come handy over there,' he said.

He had simply meant to tantalize him to squash his hopes later, but Jake was determined to follow Beatrice on their expedition as her protector.

- 'And how long have you known each other now?' he said.
- 'Three weeks?' said Jake, hesitant.
- 'Ah … Isn't that a bit early to invite yourself into her life?'
- 'But, you've just said you wanted me to come, right?' said Jake, childishly confused.

As he watches the sun go down through the panoramic alcove where the south end of the garden disappears behind the veil of darkness, he remembers how later, during the evening, Jake had left for Eden Borough and Beatrice had cloistered herself in her bedroom, or so he thought. The Everly Bothers "All I do is dream, dream, dream" was playing on the radio. Jonathan did not make anything of it at first, but once Jake had left, as he listened to his favourite show on the radio, he remembered catching sight of the golden scarab during his oneiric encounter with Osiris.

Listening to oldies-but-goodies programmes, he had felt as if he was reconnecting with his childhood and the songs his parents would listen to. As he marvelled at the tune crackling from an old vinyl from the radio DJ's collection —a remarkable feature of the nostalgic programme— he was startled by a news flash. The syrupy chorus was suddenly interrupted as he was about to dust out his vocal chords to join in:

- 'Reports are indicating that North Korea is to declare war on the UK. the PM is due to make an official announcement from number 10. Our

Westminster correspondent is outside Downing Street. Allison, are the rumours official?' said the newsreader.
- Yes Jacques, it seems that the cabinet meeting this morning was essentially about pledging support to China and Australia who have already begun talks with the Japanese PM. What we're seeing here is an unflinching determination to put a stop to the successive relentless nuclear threats on Australian soil,' said the reporter.
- 'And when can we expect an announcement to the public, Allison?
- Imminently, I should say, as I have been told there is a commotion in the hall of the PM's official residence as we speak. The newsroom let the cat out of the bag in a leaked statement this morning at 7 a.m., and the door is opening to confirm precisely that,' said the reporter.

Watching with trepid anticipation the legendary lectern being taken out, then quickly taken back in due to torrential rains, the reporter described the press being on their toes. Cameramen bustled with abnegation under the pelting deluge to shield cameras from the rain. Within a few minutes of the PM's appearance, the rain suddenly stopped, leaving the amassed crowd of journos wondering whatever the Premier could be debating with the uniformed police officer at the door:

- 'The mobile rostrum is now being placed at a reasonable distance from the news crowd, slowly and with pomp, but the police officer seems troubled. He's just turned his head away from the PM to listen to his radio feed,' described the radio reporter.

Rishi Sunak walking to his lectern, smiled awkwardly and composed himself as he lay down his dossier with a subdued facial hiatus that filled the Downing Street pool with an ominous sense of apocalypse:

- 'Why do they always say "outside Downing Street"' said Beatrice, a whiff of horse sweat and exhilaration clinging to her. She had been riding Origan whereas Jonathan thought she was cloistered in her room. 'It's dystopian saying "outside" when everyone knows they are *on* Downing Street, don't you think? What's the matter?' said Beatrice, suddenly worried about the gloomy expression on her uncle's face.

- 'There's talks of a war declaration between North Korea and the UK, please just listen!' said Jonathan.

According to the radio feed, the PM was expeditive and the announcement lasted barely three minutes:

- 'The cabinet and I have reconvened this morning after last night's news of a nuclear attack on Australian soil, the allies and the UK have now decided to enter into a crisis negotiation with North Korea. The supposed nuclear attack on Australia yesterday was part of a campaign of disinformation launched by Russia in an attempt to destabilise the alliance. We are not at war. I repeat, we are *not* at war. Thank you.'
- 'That's thick, isn't it?' blurted out Beatrice.
- 'We're still leaving. No matter what they say. It's obviously another news spin-off. In any case, we're flying to Australia to see my cousin first thing. I spoke to her last night and this morning. There hasn't been a nuclear attack on Australia.
- Is it safe though?' Beatrice whined.
- 'It hasn't been safe since the US has positioned military personel at the Ukrainian border. This mad disinformation has spread to every corner of our world. How safe is safe anyway? But I took precautions, flying to Australia and avoiding Russian soil should be okay.
- Err … is it?' argued Beatrice, striking a disjointed pose.
- 'It's time to think about our flight tomorrow night. I am not changing my plans. Do please make sure Origan and the others are all bolted in, will you? And then take a shower, call your mother. Make sure Jake is on standby. We shan't be delayed by your boyfriend.
- Uncle, Jake is *not* my boyfriend! How many times do I have to say it?
- You, young people and your boundaries, I mean, we all know where this is going. I am a man, I sure know what's on his mind!' said Jonathan.
- 'Jake is probably gay, Uncle. I am not quite sure yet, and I don't care!' said Beatrice.

Beatrice stood firmly in the doorway, in her muddy boots, determined to settle the dispute. Deadstone smiled at her riding gear, expecting a scene with relish.

- 'Your mood is quite daunting, Unk. I have to say,' said Beatrice.
- 'Is it? I am just saying that there's uncertainty already, we can't possibly have a defector! Last time you spoke to him, he was undecided,' said Jonathan.
- 'What? When? I really don't need this, right now! Jake is evasive about his plans? Tough!
- 'He's so working class! I mean, have you seen his old trainers?' said Jonathan.

She meant to gesture reprisal with the Jack Hardy, but instead found herself chasing a fly.

- 'It's in his nature to be like that, Unk. It has nothing to do with his social status.
- Well, I don't want yet another episode of the Archers tonight. We are expected in Japan in two weeks. I have been preparing our itinerary for two months now!' he said.
- 'I know, and you haven't told us how you plan to travel from Australia to Japan yet.
- Is he seriously coming with us, Bee?
- I wouldn't have it any other way,' said Beatrice.

Beatrice didn't expect her uncle to lay still with his feet entangled around his knees in levitation at the news Jake was part of the trip. Yet, she couldn't help picturing the scene of their happiness on a Japanese mountain top, contemplating the next nuclear war unfolding with Jake at their side.

- 'Adventure on, we must … I guess!' yielded Jonathan.

Epitath for a Chimpanzee

The departed Charles was buried below a sycamore tree with a plaque to commemorate his life's works. Jonathan Deadstone had been looking for something in the vein of Lord Byron's epitaph for his dog. But, at the last minute, Deadstone decided Charles deserved better:

'According to the laws of men,
Few can claim their prize to Glory.
But here rests a monkey.
Whose selflessness was returned in specie.'

Satisfied with his valediction, Deadstone laid his companion to rest, in a shaded spot by an oak tree. During the ceremony, Beatrice tried to probe his Saturn state of late:

- 'Uncle, are you okay with Jake coming with us? Since the beginning, you have been weird like.
- Oh, no. Absolutely not, I'm glad we have a photographer on board!' said Jonathan.
- 'I think he's also taking his video equipment. Cool, right?' said Beatrice.
- 'Well, of course, the more the merrier. I just hope he will be parsimonious with the side effects.'

They both laughed, yet with a tear in their eyes for the monkey. But Deadstone was determined to keep his darkest thoughts secret. Somehow, he could not help thinking that, in the eyes of Beatrice, Jake was a sad trade-off for Charles. This sordid thought curiously cheered him up as he auto-analysed his grieving psyche.

"Grief is a wondrous feeling," he thought, as he saw Beatrice texting frantically from the corner of his eye, trying to settle his mind about the journey ahead and the obstacles authorities could lay on their path. He suddenly felt a craving for salty foods. He even pictured himself sitting on a Japanese knoll, eating crisps while Beatrice was massaging his feet. He didn't entirely dismiss the thought of a female monk (he'd never seen any) fanning his upper body with a large palm leaf.

- 'Are you coming?' said Beatrice under the lulling oak, 'The wind is rising.'

He thought with satisfaction that there would be none of that mobile technology at the top of Tomurauchi mountain, which he had warned Beatrice about, except perhaps for the cameras, the optics and travelling gear, such as compass and GPS. Couldn't escape that malarkey. Now that they were close to each other again, the thought of abandoning Charles to an empty manor made his lips quirk. He immediately extracted himself from the very same thought: Charles was dead. He knew those little epiphanies would string along like a festoon at at New Orleans funeral until reality and his grief finally aligned. "Grief is a wondrous thing", he thought while Beatrice gawped at him:

- 'Do you believe monkeys have a spirit, Uncle?
- Hmmm? Of course, they do, all animals have,' he said distractedly.
- 'Unk, I am really glad we're travelling together.
- So am I, sweetie.'

Under the neo-classical porch of his manor house, Jonathan Deadstone looked at Beatrice with the eyes of a man who saw a beautiful woman for the first time. Beatrice's langorous eyes seemed to return his thoughts with magical synchronicity. She now knew that her uncle was in love with her …

Plain as Plane

- 'You look serious as a heart attack, Bee … What are you reading?' asked Jake.
- 'It's the Megillah of all mandalas, if you wanna know …The what?'

Beatrice giggled …

- 'Wisdom-seekers, up and comers like you and me are travelling inside a mandala to find the way to a sacred flower … It looks like a map,' said Jake, peering over her shoulder.

Jake cooped, snooping on Beatrice's book. It had a blue and gold cover, a star sign encapsulating a central flower on the cover.

- 'I'm at the point where the monk turns into a snail and hides to everyone's eyes.
- Oh … ' said Jake, disappointed.

Beatrice turned pages with a comforting ruffle, amidst the purring of engines, the clamour of whispering voices, the stamping of travellers feet on the carpeted floor of the plane, the squeak of plastic seats and the nearly imperceptible creaking of the plane's fuselage …

- 'Still, it's creepy that the book should be about a flower …Hmmm?' Beatrice turned to stare at Jake.
- 'Duh … Can't you see? We're going to Japan so your uncle can see a flower on a mountain, and you're reading a book about a flower?' said Jake.

Beatrice sighed, her mind obviously wandering off to the story she was reading.

- 'Yeah ... It's not the same kind of flower, though,' she said.

But the crackle of audio in his headphones scrambled his ideas for a conversation. He turned off the video sound. Beatrice was visibly entranced by her book and wouldn't be easily distracted. Instead, Jake listened to the trail of his own thoughts. How they materialised from feelings into emotions, as Jonathan had told him they would during their tête-à-tête in his library. How interesting, Jake thought, that he should have feelings that could be turned into words, into whole stories ...

"There is no mind. What we call the mind is an illusion. Memory, neuronal connections carry electrical signals. It's a physical phenomenon. The meaning of those connections and the impact they have on our various bodily systems create the illusion that we think. It gives our thoughts dimension we think we comprehend. Atmospheric pressure creates the illusion that memory is a place in the mind. In fact, the effect of gravity on our senses means our body sensors are always scouring for remnants of light. There is no mind ... What we see, hear, feel is traceable only because it is designed to be memorised according to programmed parameters. Our brain's inability to comprehend the unknown is called the mind. A whole new way of living life," he thought.

- 'Jake, I'm done reading,' said Beatrice.

Jake opened his eyes to hers, whose face was closer to his now.

- 'Oh ... Now, you are!' he said.
- 'What are you listening to?' asked Beatrice.
- 'Nothing actually. I was just thinking ...About what?
- About the present and whatever.
- Anti-matter?
- Yeah ... ' Jake snorted. 'So how was your book?
- I am in the middle of it, it's exciting, just two teenagers, a boy and a girl on an adventure inside a mandala. Lots of strange encounters with

strange characters, a bit like Alice in Wonderland, but for adults. It's very interesting,' said Beatrice.

A stewardess walked past. She was wearing a bicolour uniform that looked like an open red page on a black book. Classy, but incisive, mordant, yet tacky and desperately outdated, the uniform underlined her red lipstick. Beatrice sighed …

- 'Do you miss your dad, Bee?
- Sometimes …How old were you when he died?
- I was 15 … I told you … I was in high school, year 11 …Sorry, I didn't mean to make you sad …Nah, don't worry. It's been three years and half already.
- What about you, do you miss your mum?
- Yes, sometimes. I wish she had known you,' said Jake.
- 'Oh, that's very nice. I am chuffed,' said Beatrice, beaming.

They both looked through the window. Jake robbed a glance at the tuft candy flower on Beatrice's sleeves rubbing against his leg. They watched the clouds lined with golden streaks of honeyed sunshine:

- 'It's only two hours to Melbourne,' said Jake, 'When do you think we'll get to Japan? I'm seriously looking forward to it. After reading those Mangas, I hope I can visit a game arcade. It should be well cool.
- Yeah, me too. We'll have time to do whatever we want, hopefully,' said Beatrice, plumping her lips as she leant on Jake's shoulder.
- 'Your uncle seems bored … Should you go and talk to him?
- Oh, no … He's okay, I saw him writing on his notebook a few minutes ago, while you were sleeping, he's probably watching a ballbuster movie with a snatched twink yassy main character,' said Beatrice. They laughed loudly.

Water, Stones and Wax

Jonathan was facing his sculptural self in the mirror, wondering if Beatrice would like his new look, or if the jetlag was simply distorting his perception of his charms ...

He pondered his childish jealousy towards Jake and his involvement with Beatrice, the object of his persistent fantasy. He had observed the two of them on the plane, how they rubbed off each other, jostling amorously at time, like two puerile teenagers, or mimicking amorous adult behaviour, getting all somber and discussing grown-up stuff. But Beatrice wasn't a child nor a teenager any more and her eighteen-year-old body challenged his principled mind.

Since their departure from Scotland, the idea of a beard had grown on him. He looked vacantly at his jetlag bags. They were unpacked, dark with realism. His eyes, heavy with the shadow of the foul dilemma he was now inhabiting, struggled to find his beard sexy. The ground floor room at Jackie's guest house was looking out onto a beautifully maintained garden, where a tuckeroo tree, rhaphiolepis, yellow marigolds and orange crocosmias, among various tropical plants, painted a paradisial picture.

Jackie was a cousin of the Hallmarks. Her likeness with Catherine had stunned Beatrice. She had never met her before and found the resemblance with her mother uncanny. Fortunately for her, unlike her narcissistic mother, Jackie, a freckled middle-aged blond with a large pearly white smile was grounded and caring.

Jackie had dropped the post that had come in for him. Dubois' letter had been posted from the City of Shirataka in Japan, where he was expecting their arrival and that of the psychotherapist and keen adventurer, Roger Doherty, a seasoned practitioner of the art of Wu Wei or the Chinese Taoist concept of letting things happen. Leaving it to chance is what Wu Wei was all about, explained Dubois. What would it look like if it were applied to him, he pondered. What if he let things happen without hindrance?

His enactment of the possible romantic scenarios involving Beatrice? Yielding to his uncontrollable lust, behaving like a child eager to be punished for his brazen thoughts? Beatrice was the object of his desires, and the feeling was raw and simple. He had to look at it a different way. What would the enactment of his overwhelming desire look like in reality?

All things considered, life was smiling on him again. For a moment, he felt like the leukemia was behind him. It's as if, his attraction to Beatrice had relegated his own mortal disease at the back of his mind. Dubois had said that the Everblue would make his disease all seem like a bad dream. He had to ponder his next moves now that he found himself trapped between inane hope and reckless abandonment. Visiting Beatrice's bedroom last night was definitely out of line. He had convinced himself that a fatherly need for reassurance should prevail over his shamefacedness. But the mirror was now relentlessly debunking the myth of his eternal youth.

Flowing deep undercurrent, in his shadow mind, the prospect of her defloration had become a fixation since they arrived in Australia, as if the distance between her mother and her meant he had now free reins to use her as he pleased. He checked his alibis, feeling gratified by the smell of his beard ointment. Among the dark current of possessiveness that gelled with his blue sky thinking, a juvenile bubbling anticipation was resurfacing in his life like a shark. And that one didn't need justification. Under the clement Australian weather, the thrilling sensation of possessing her youthful body had now become too delightful to repress. In this adventurous atmosphere, their collective excitement would be a fertile ground to make his fantasies come true.

Facing the mirror with the minty fragrance of his beard ointment, he suddenly struggled to stomach the truth: the Everblue was the vanishing point of all fantasies. His body suddenly felt like a ghost ship scouring the shore for a port to call. What if she turned him down? He couldn't help relishing the thought that no matter how much he would delay his fantasy by spicing it up with the thought of the act itself, he would have to explain his feelings with the risk of estranging her. Jonathan sighed responsibly. The journey promised to be even more excruciating than he had thought. Now that the reality of his transgression felt more imperious, more embodied and fuller, so the reward was bound to be sweeter.

Jake and Beatrice had gone trekking around Melbourne to fight off the jetlag. In the morning, Jonathan would book three seats on a plane to Tokyo, Japan. At dinner, he would let them know what the plan was.

Wu Wei, or the art of letting things happen …

Just like water is fluid, feminine and free to run wild, he would let his fantasies run amok for now until they found the stone of his widowed heart. In the sunny February sun, breathing the new air to the full capacity of his lungs, he therefore found himself facing an antipodal self, for whom change was scary and dangerous. Although he looked down on Doherty's psychospiritual discipline as poshed-up quackery, the idea of letting things take their course without influencing them had a certain charm.

Roger Doherty: professor of the art of flow, of wild running water against the rocks of ego.

But for Jonathan, the stone was bleeding and water had been replaced by whiskey. If he liked the idea of "wu weing" his way to Beatrice's virginity at the first opportunity, he felt that the ship of surrogacy that he had steered conscientiously after Beatrice's father's death had to sail. She deserved his full love. No one was better suited than him to steer the precious Jasper of her innocence to safety.

He poured himself a drink and finished reading the letter from Dubois, satisfied with this new outlook on his sexual desire.

He immediately felt the ominous truth running through the anthropologist's handwriting, like a stark warning between the lines, something in the vein of "The Eye was in the Tomb". Biblical scaremongering aside, from the ink and paper oozed a strange aura that soon gelled in his brain to form an omen, as if the writing had been on the wall of this small Australian family pension all the time.

If the thought of challenging his amorous plans ever occurred to him, the letter dismissed it straight away. Superstition aside, why was Dubois letting on that he knew next to nothing about the location of the flower? Jonathan settled into the hotel room arm chair, with its neutral pastel and impersonal patterns, and read on, making sure that there was no contact between his skin and the bedding and soft furnishing textile, as a hygienic precaution. The Covid pandemic had been declared. He knew better than to risk a viral infection in his state.

It wasn't the first time Jonathan had a strange esoteric intuition that challenged his rational mind. In fact, the psychotherapist Doherty had triggered similar suspicions on their first encounter. But he had rather pictured the psychospiritual guru in diapers practising Tai Chi among clapping kangoroos than to take his presence on the expedition seriously. He wouldn't be an obstacle to his plans. When push came to shove, he would argue that punching the impostor in the face was Wu Wei as much as anything else. What with the jet lag, his bearded impersonation seemed ruthless.

Of course, as a psychiatrist, Jung, Laing, Freud, Stein and the tribe of psychologists that had followed the 1970s drug culture were on his side. Jonathan had payed tribute to their legacy and emulated their shitfaced exploits himself in his time, but Doherty's particular brand of aristocratic and navelist psychology could prove a sticking point between them. He had vetoed his mumbo-jumbo immediately: *Had he looked closer into his own discipline*, ranted Jonathan, muttering to himself, *Doherty would probably have noticed that the cult he professed as a spiritual experiment was just childish overcompensation for post-Hiroshima nihilism.*

Besides announcing Doherty's arrival in Shirataka, at the foot of Mount Asahi, Dubois also included more information about the Everblue. As Japan got nearer, Jonathan would find out if the flower that blew men's consciousness was anything more than a distraction for the fun-employed. He couldn't wait for his circles of consciousness to expand … In his frenzied mind, the thought of skipping his chemotherapy treatment did also occur to him, but for now, with the delays in the NHS service and the fact he could administer the drip himself, the makeshift drip from a saline bag, hooked up to the old-fashioned coat hanger in his hotel room, while the kids were out rambling, would be good enough for now.

Dubois had arranged for the services of a guide, who was also a monk. He had scoured the region to find the village where he and Master Khul had spent their mystical days. But the flower had been traced to another region, in Hokkaido, near Mount Asahi … Jonathan was bemused. What's with the change of location? Did the Everblue have legs too? Yet another monk, why?

The situation with North Korea was dismal according to Dubois. A long-range rocket had been launched to test a ballistic missile which flew right over the supposed location of the Everblue. Dubois was goading the expeditonists by ending his letter with a drawing of the flower. *That should settle the question whether Dubois was ever in contact with the flower or not*, thought Jonathan. Then again, his drawing could have been based on the monk's recollection. The mystery remained entire …Jonathan pocketed the letter and went down to the dining room where Jackie and her staff were busy serving a dozen of guests at their table. A young Russian soldier was playing piano excitedly, showing off his scales without any recognisable sense of rhythm. He caught him leering intermittently towards the table where Beatrice and Jake were already waiting for their food.

Beatrice was seeping a shiraz wine thoughtfully. The desperado mien of the piano player had attracted her attention. His dishevelled style, his lyrical intepretations of the sheets spread haphazardly on the rack, painted a sordid picture that constrasted starkly with the home feel of the guest house. She saw him stooped over his scales, listening distractedly to his attempts at jazzing up swing standards with a hurriedness that made her think he didn't want to be there. She was smiling wistfully.

As he sat down, Jonathan gasped at her short black lace dress that revealed her tanned body. While they were waiting for the evening barbecue razzmatazz, Jake entertained the table with his doom's day view of the world post-climate change, bearing on the table's mood like the grim reaper. But Jonathan couldn't keep his eyes from Beatrice's dazzling beauty. Her complexion and bare arms were like golden fruits. For him, she was a juicy orange bursting with zest. He felt goosebumps, letting his mind wu wei to more tufty areas of her body, suddenly feeling the insistent stare of the piano player who couldn't stop ogling at her between over-lyrical scales. Jonathan glanced at him disapprovingly.

Beatrice's charms weren't lost on Jake either. Jonathan knew full well why Jake's eyes had a different texture all of sudden. They were oiled, lubricated with sexual intent. Jonathan was pondering whether her pheronomes were not part of this collective illusion when Jackie came to lay a dish of gambas on the table, straight from the inferno of the barbecue:

- 'You look wonderful tonight, Beatrice. Enjoy your dinner, everyone!'

Jonathan neatly placed a napkin on his lap, while Jackie dutifully turned her attention to other guests.

- 'So, children, I have good news for you! Our visas have arrived. We are going to Japan tomorrow! We're driving to Sydney to take a flight to

Tokyo, then by train to a different city, where we will stay over for a couple of days, before catching another train to the foot of the mountain.
- Seriously, that soon? But we'd planned to go to the beach with some friends we met on the trails, didn't we Jake?' said Beatrice, as if she had found a fly in the ointment.
- 'So, you're not coming, I take it?' said Jonathan, blithely.
- 'Of course I am coming! I can't think of anything more thrilling than to spend a few weeks on the coldest mountains in Japan' she retorted wittingly.
- 'Oh, well, it's not as cold in April, besides, it's now or never, if we wait longer, we risk missing the blooming season. I suspect the Everblue is a kind of primrose, or an early spring bloomer. So we'd better not delay,' said Jonathan.
- 'Can we visit Tokyo, at least?' asked Beatrice, pouting her lips.
- 'I am afraid not. There's no time for that. Sorry, darling.'
- 'But what are we looking for exactly?' she asked.
- 'Oh, yeah, I was going to ask you the same,' said Jake candidly.
- 'As I told you, Bee, the expedition must remain a secret, until we know for sure what we're looking for and where,' said Jonathan.

He glanced at Jake sideways.

- 'I am totally up for it, but I have a schedule unfortunately, I must earn some Wonga,' pre-empted Jake, in his customed straightforwardness.

Jonathan gave him another reproving look, which Jake returned with alacrity.

- 'Which reminds me, our friends from Wagga Wagg,' said Beatrice.
- 'The plunkers, right?' added Jake.
- 'Yeah … ' chuckled Beatrice.
- 'So rude, but in a funny way … Right?' said Jake.
- 'Yeah, pretty rough Sheila, what was her name?' said Beatrice.
- 'Debbie!' said Jake.
- 'Oh, yeah, that's right!' They both laughed.

- 'So, where are we going, I forgot?' asked Beatrice, swallowing a piece of gamba, interrogating Jonathan with her mouth open onto a pink morsel of masticated food.
- 'We are off tomorrow to Yokohama, at the first hour, well, after a nice breakie, of course, we should not forget our manners,' said Jonathan, responsibly.
- 'As long as it's all free, I'm game for anything really, hot or cold,' said Jake, contentedly.
- 'Jake sure seems like a lesser burden now that we can count on him to carry the luggage,' joked Beatrice, complicitly.

They both rebuked each other playfully. Again, as he walked back to his guest room, after a warm embrace with Jackie, he couldn't help thinking that his attraction to Beatrice would soon need an outlet. He felt an ominous sense of compassion for her, especially after reading Dubois's letter. But, under extreme conditions, he was confident he would know what to do. *Three is a crowd nevertheless*, he thought …The next morning felt like summer in February, which it was. Jonathan felt the heat as soon as he woke up. As he had omitted to switch on the air conditioner in his room, his Scottish skin found the temperature uncomfortable and he noticed many red blotches besides his profuse sweating. They had to find the Everblue in spring, rather than in summer, let alone winter. Which meant that, if Jonathan and Beatrice could stay longer than the month originally planned, as he expected they would, Jake would soon be out of the way. All in all, this morning had brought glad tidings …The flights from Sydney to Tokyo had now been booked. From there, the schedule was a short journey to Yokohama, then a train from Yokohama to Shirataka, the village at the foot of Mount Asahi … He breakfasted alone and checked out. The chauffeur from Melbourne arrived on time. The meeting point was the guest house entrance.

- 'Are they gonna be any longer?' said a bald-headed Arabian chauffeur, sitting on the edge of his car seat, one foot outside the well. He had been waiting for around ten minutes.
- 'They shouldn't be too long now, I'll check the rooms,' Jonathan decided.

He called from reception but neither of the rooms answered. He tried a second time asking the black receptionnist lunging in an armchair in a flowery dress to check a third time. Without any answer, she crossed her legs behind the counter and asked irreverently if he wanted to check the rooms himself.

- 'Can't you send someone at least? I am afraid the driver will let me down, he's already impatient,' said Jonathan.
- 'I can ask one of the caretakers to have a look, but I'm not sure if they're on the same level, sir. Besides, Jackie is away today. I am only covering,' said the receptionist.
- 'Ask them to level up, then, I am in a bit of a pickle here, we're going to Sidney for a 10 p.m. check-in!'

On second thoughts, he rushed to the stairs to check Beatrice's room himself. It was on the third floor. He needed the exercise. Building up frantic and excrutiating scenarios about Jake and Beatrice having sex in a graveyard for a reason he could not understand, he felt the blood rush to his temples. He got to the third floor, caught his breath and knocked on the door. The timer in the corridor kept switching the lights on and off.

- 'Where is she?' he grumbled, pacing up and down the corridor.

There was no answer. After five minutes, he came downstairs again and saw Jake through the veranda, twiddling a branch of eucalyptus.

- 'Ah, there you are!' said Jonathan.

Beatrice stepped out from behind a Eucalyptus tree. She had been holding Jake's hand but let go of it when she saw her uncle:

- 'Hi, Unk!' she said.
- 'Where were you? Did you even sleep in your room last night?' he asked, trying to sound caring …
- 'Er … ' said Jake.
- 'Jake, don't,' she said.

Beatrice put off her cigarette.

- 'Do you smoke now? What's with all the secrecy?' said Jonathan.

She shook her head, blowing out smoke.

- 'No secrets. We spent the night out with friends, we ended up in a graveyard for some reason, don't ask me how,' said Beatrice.

Jonathan was puzzled. Jake turned his head away, commenting on the beautiful sunshine.

- 'Let's get going,' said Jonathan, fuming.

A few minutes into the journey, as the atmosphere in the minivan became uncomfortable, even with a sharp knife, Beatrice complained she had rather they had caught a plane.

- 'I wanted you to see some of the countryside. Besides, we have plenty of time,' said Jonathan.

The Melbourne suburbs soon vanished behind red-brown expanses of semi-arid wastelands, then scrubby plains, then lush fields on the banks of rivers. The passengers fell silent again, gawping at the strange scenery.

- 'What a stark difference with the City,' said Jake, knowledgeably.

'It reminds me of that old belting "Plane!" movie, where the pilot walks aimlessly out of the US city pondering his dilemna, eyes on his feet, and the next thing you know, he finds himself in a leafy tropical jungle surrounded by exotic sounds.'

But no one found Jake's joke funny.

- 'Is anyone going to tell me what on earth you've been up to last night, for God's sake?' said Jonathan in a galled outburst.

- 'The journey's gonna be fun,' said Jake, scratching his forehead.

Beatrice was dozing off, on the back seat.

- 'I think she's asleep, John, you know,' said Jake.

Jonathan glanced at Jake sideways. He too fell silent. Jonathan tried to recollect his thoughts and plan the rest of the journey in his head, avoiding the reprobating gaze of the driver in the mirror. Mid-journey, Beatrice emerged from her sobering sleep.

- 'Yeah, we spent the night in a graveyard,' she said.

Jake and Beatrice had been out all night, meeting up with friends after a nightclub spree. Americans on a backpack tour of Eastern Asia. They had spent the rest of the night in a graveyard, drinking and sneering at death.

- 'Oh, did you now?' grumbled Jonathan. The chauffeur chuckled.
- 'Yes, we met them at a pub. There was a rock band playing,' said Jake.
- 'Oh yeah, which band?' the driver asked, mundanely interested.

Jonathan kept an open mind. After all, Beatrice knew better than to give herself that easily, especially in a graveyard …

- 'A cover band, actually. They were playing ACDC stuff. But we didn't stay long, it wasn't our vibe. The Americans felt the same, so we went to that nightclub instead,' said Beatrice.
- 'How did you end up in a graveyard?' asked Jonathan, concerned.
- 'Just chatting, enjoying the world of spirits, Australian style,' she said.

Jake snorted at her remark.

- 'Oh, yeah? And … What was it like down under there?' asked Jonathan.
- 'To be frank, it wasn't spooky or anything, we were just chilling. We just drank some beers and before you know it, it was time for breakfast, right Jake?

- Yup. Lovely breakfast it was too,' said Jake.
- What became of the Americans, did you part company?' asked Jonathan, hair-raised.
- No, they're in the boot,' said Jake.
- 'What's that Jake?' Jonathan suppressed a nervous outburst. The driver chuckled.
- 'But they're flying to Yokohama too. In fact, their next leg is Sapporo, it's up north from where we're going, so they will probably join us,' said Beatrice candidly.
- 'They what?' said Jonathan.

Jonathan turned around so brusquely that the driver jolted back into his seat.

- 'You did what, Bee?' he said.

She paused for a few seconds, measuring what she had said, hesitantly:

- 'I ... just told them we were on an expedition. They seemed interested, so I kept their numbers. No harm done. I didn't give out mine, don't worry!
- Yep, Taylor's, from Cambridge, Massachusetts,' Jake added, shrugging and rolling his eyes.
- 'Can you stop the minivan, please?' Jonathan asked, infuriated.

The driver in front nodded and cleared his throat:

- 'Yes, at the next stop, mate, we're only a few miles away.
- Staggering!' exploded Jonathan, 'Do you realise how compromised this expedition could be if ... if ...Oh, bother! I won't call him, then. I just thought it would make the expedition more fun, that's all,' said Beatrice.
- 'Now, Mister Deadstone, I can testify. They were very prude all night,' said Jake.
- 'You shut your pipe hole, Jake!' Beatrice said, feigning irritation.

Jake and Beatrice looked at each other in connivance. The driver shrugged. Jake shrugged too, imitating the driver and smiling, he looked at Jonathan's face in the mirror and gave him an exagerrated simper. Beatrice also smiled, albeit sheepishly. Jonathan was now looking vacantly at the scenery, sulking and sullen, behind the driver.The journey went on without further arguments or questioning. Jonathan felt it was best to leave it until Sidney to find out more about Taylor and the night at the graveyard. As promised, the driver stopped at Jugiong, a petrol station in the middle of nowhere. As soon as the engine stopped, Jake raised his head, looking around the deserted truckstop. He and Jonathan came out of the minivan to look at the lacklustre roadhouse's front and its narrow arrow-hole vertical windows. A hay runner was leaving the car park. They looked at each other, dulled by the inconspicuous scenery:

- 'What a shithole!' said Jake.
- 'There are a couple of graveyards, if you fancy,' said the driver, sniggering.

Jonathan made a beeline for the loo without talking to them.

- 'Shall we see what food is on offer?' asked Jake.
- 'Yeah, you go ahead, I'll be visiting a friend in the village, down the road, we're back on the road in an hour,' said the driver, scuttling away.
- 'Okay,' said Jake, hands in his black jeans' pockets, 'See you later.'

Jonathan had rushed off in anger, Jake saw his decided gait disappear inside the roadhouse's toilets.

- 'He's well cross,' Jake muttered to himself.

Once inside the restaurant, Jake ordered a beer and chatted with the staff. A young lad with a week's stub, who manipulated the beer tap with a pitiful air of resignation, engaged with him in casual conversation. Jake eyed a Chesterfield sofa, by a cold woodfire, in the opposite corner of the roadhouse, looking past Beatrice without seeing her.

Beatrice watched Jake as he was about to come back from the bar. As if hypnotised by the washed-out interior of the dunghole in the middle of nowhere, she combed her long strawberry blond hair with her fingers. The couple of truckers at the end of the bar were still, looking towards her dull-eyedly. Jake seemed frozen, his hand reaching over the counter. She noticed Kaolin patterns smudged on his face. She saw herself walking towards the entrance door to the sound of a didgeridoo, a strange feeling of lightness in her movement, as the door opened in front of her, automatically. She couldn't see Jonathan anywhere now that she was outside, looking in. She remembered the driver's words and walked in the direction of a graveyard, noticing the eery absence of sounds around her, and then, walking past a deserted junk yard and disused post down the road, found herself peering into a misty valley, down over the road embankment. She returned to the café, as if by magic, unsure how long she had spent wandering, or if what she had just seen was real or not, to find Jake arguing with truckers. A lorry had capzised and the local hay runner had towed them out of the ditch, according to their distant, but strangely now louder conversation. Beatrice suddenly felt the atmosphere in the little anodyne café had changed, as she sat on the edge of the Chesterfield sofa, puzzled at their unexplainable argument. Jake was visibly excited and loquacious. Maybe, he had had a few beers and the heat had gotten to him. The truckers seemed ostentatiously annoyed at his overbearing jubilant dribble and cheeky demeanour. Beatrice picked up the Chicko wrap he had left for her on the seat and munched mechanically, watching the scene unfold. Suddenly, she heard the sound of breaking glass …What she saw next, now standing by the car, was Jake being manhandled by the truckers. One of them was behind him, holding her friend's arms while the other slapped him violently on the cheeks. Beatrice was shocked. She felt like running to find Jonathan, but instead kept finding herself by the car, looking around, beserk on the car park. She heard the argument spilling over on to the dusty lay-by and saw Jake coming out of the restaurant with blood on his face. The truckers were mandhandling him, and as Jake tried to flee, caught up with him. Jake tried to extricate himself from their stronghold, rustling with their powerful hold, when one of them pushed him violently to the ground. Jake fell and tried to stand up on his feet, but as the adrenaline kicked in, he stood up to face both of them, challenging them to a fight.

- 'You wanker! Come on then! Is that all you've got, cowards?' Jake shouted, threatening them with his fists.

Jake was blurbing comments about some inbred dynasty of truckers that scoured the Australian countryside.

- 'Jake!' Beatrice shouted.

Jake came to his senses, turned towards Beatrice, realised the absurdity of the situation and scurried towards her. But one of the truckers followed him, produced a knife and ran it through Jake's back as he meant to run towards her. Beatrice, horrified, crossed eyes with Jake as he fell to the ground. He held a hand out to her and opened his mouth to speak …

- 'We're here now,' said the minivan driver, in front of Sidney airport.

Beatrice woke up, both groggy and startled, a grid of furnishing textile from the minivan seat printed red on her cheek.

- 'Now, I need to give you your tickets,' said Jonathan, opening his door hurriedly. 'Bee, I need to talk to you, in private!'
- 'What? No, I'm starving,' said Beatrice, emerging from her sobering sleep.
- 'It's your fault, you conked out in the desert,' said Jake, jovially.
- 'Yes, we didn't want to wake you up at the Roadhouse. Wait here, I'll get you some food,' said Jonathan, paternally.

Beatrice needed a minute to shake herself out of her bad dream. She stayed in the minivan to take stock. Once they all stepped out and thanked the driver, Beatrice let out a sigh of relief, stretching her legs as Jake helped the driver taking the luggage out of the boot.

- 'Take it easy, Jonathan,' the driver said balefully.
- 'Thanks for driving, driver,' Jonathan said standoffishly.

The check-in line at the airport was dense. As Jake sat on his photographic equipment cases, Jonathan took Beatrice aside:

- 'You and I need a chat. I sent you dozens of texts waiting for you this morning! This can't happen in Japan. You can't speak a word of Japanese, besides, what came over you to spend the night in a graveyard with complete strangers? I am responsible for your safety, and I was worried sick last night, so you know! I checked your bedroom this morning. I thought something bad had happened to you. You have to be a bit more responsible, Bee.'

Beatrice stormed off, ignoring Jonathan.

- 'Where are you going to?
- I'm going to get myself a drink, I am so parched! I just had the most stupid nightmare!' she said.

She ambled listlessly back to the entrance doors.

- 'Beatrice!' Jonathan followed her in her footsteps and stopped in her tracks, holding her arm. 'Wait! What is wrong?
- I am so annoyed at what you said in the car! How can you think I would tell anyone about the expedition? I just took the guy's number. No big deal,' said Beatrice.

She battered her eyelids, gasping in disbelief.

- 'I am not saying you did, Bee, but I was worried, that's all. We need to keep a line of communication open if you intend to elope with Jake, next time. I know he's your friend, but I find him very opportunistic and reckless! It's not like you to walk off like this. Now is it?'

Beatrice pondered his remark. An effortless expression of indignation tainted with scepticism is what he thought he saw.

- 'I am an adult, you know!
- I know, and you look it too! But, I can't help thinking that if something happened to you, I couldn't bear it. If you … '

Jonathan felt the moment was ripe to tell her how he really felt, but his eyes wandered …

- 'Hey, relax, I get it … You've been looking at me with different eyes, lately, Unk. Don't worry, I am not judging … I promise you I won't endanger myself,' she said.

She perked her breasts, straightening her spine, conscious his temperamental behaviour was due to his repressed desire for her.

- 'I love you, you know?' said Jonathan.
- 'I know,' she said, stroking his arm.

She smiled at him wistfully. He felt a rush of masculine pride overtaking his body, primed as if filled with the flavours of a new breeze that was blowing over his face and the sky above so blue that sunshine seemed to inundate his heart with loving warmth.

Fishbowl Psychology

Sea paradise. Koy fish-fingers, autistic love. A Japanese fish tank gallery with variegated snug holes teeming with life: theirs eyes wandered in the amniotic world of genesis around them. The sea world's weird eyes swallowed theirs: angelfish, starfish, gobies, seahorses and gaudy remnants of light bursting through the deepest darkness of the oceans. They both marvelled at the overwhelming display of colours and shapes. But for Beatrice and Jake, the day wasn't over yet. Yokohama had so much to offer. They started with the gigantic aquarium, where all prisms of fish life were displayed in their native environment, lit with splendid and multi-coloured leds. They stopped at a puffed-up blowfish to exchange a few exclamations about its incredible poisonous organs, "a delicacy that unless prepared by a specialist chef, could kill you," Beatrice read. Jake too had heard the story. But Jake became hungry.

- 'There's a restaurant that makes bubble drinks, shall we investigate?' said Beatrice.
- 'I was about to suggest the same,' said Jake.
- 'Wow, it's mind-blowing, isn't it? All those dark shark eyes looking at food they can't touch, it must be excruciating for them!
- Have you seen how the guys who feed the white albino orcas were literally dwarfed by them?
- Just follow the whiffs to the restaurant,' joked Beatrice.

They chuckled in unison, breathing the mid-morning air, among the immensity of the sea paradise. Once in the Bubble restaurant, the thought of eating fish felt repulsive to Beatrice, as she sympathised with the poor creatures whom she thought had been unfairly deprived of their habitat. Jake tried to reassure her that they wouldn't know any better. He was trying to decipher the Japanese-English translation of the food menu when he heard a familiar voice …

He turned around to locate its origin. He recognized Doherty's voice. The man was weaving through the throng of hungry queuers back towards the aquarium like a pink salmon. Jake hesitated between following his instinct and queuing for food.

- 'Hey, Bee, I think I've just seen Doherty!
- How do you know? Did he see us?
- I dunno … I recognized his voice from the recording your uncle played.
- Let's follow him …Huh? What about the food?
- You won't die for a few minutes, will you?'

They followed Doherty back to the aquarium, showing their passes to the smiling female attendant in a blue and red uniform, wearing a red scarf around her neck.

- 'I love the quality of their clothes,' whispered Beatrice, keeping an eye on Doherty's chubby waistline as he was swallowed up into the dark sharks tunnel.
- What if it's not him?' said Jake.

They stopped short of a curved wall marking the entrance to the next display, tiptoeing their way towards the spot where the tall round-bellied hippy-yappy turned spiritual guru seemed to be waiting, looking around for someone he was seemingly expecting. Beatrice and Jake watched him pace up and down in front of the blowfish tank, giggling.

- 'I'm sure he saw us,' whispered Beatrice.
- 'He doesn't know who we are, Bee. The Angel fish, Bee, look how transparent they are … Shush, he's meeting up with someone now … Who?' Jake whispered loudly.
- 'Taylor!' babbled Beatrice.

They both glanced at them, over the curve of a display partition.

- 'They're too far, we can't hear what they're saying,' whispered Beatrice, despondent.

- 'No, look, there's a full class of high school students coming this way, you wear black and white like them, hide among them like a predator fish and then, cross over to that interactive thingy over there, look!' said Jake.
- 'I'm not. I'm wearing marine blue and white!' said Beatrice.
- 'Close enough, right?' said Jake.
- 'Okay,' said Beatrice.

Like Ulysses escaping from the cave of the giant, Beatrice blended in with the gaggle of excited students in black and white uniforms. She crossed over the hall and hid in a recess, between barracudas and dog fishes. Taylor, the young American from Massachussets, whom she had met in Melbourne, seemed to know Doherty.

- 'Thank God for that beautiful spirit that cut through all the horseshit,' said Taylor.

Beatrice perceived a sickly subservient tone in his voice, as if he feared Doherty's opinion.

- 'Anything that will boost their ego with fanciful notions of plentifulness has to become the weapon of their demise!
- She's the one, isn't she, Master?
- She is she … When the time comes, she must be abducted. You'll have no choice but to follow us on the mountain and act fast and surreptitiously.
- I am at your command, Master.
- Meet me in Shirataka, tomorrow! I'll send you the details!' said Doherty.

As he saw the two men split up, Jake hesitated. But soon, they were out of sight and he joined Beatrice by the blowfish tank. Beatrice, ashen-faced, looked like a haggard angel in the whiteness of the neon light.

- 'You look like you've seen a ghost,' said Jake.
- 'Taylor is a cult member!' said Beatrice, gasping in front of the Koy fish tank.

- 'A what?
- A member of a sect or a cult, I don't know. He calls Doherty "Master". You were right!'

They walked towards the exit and back into the daylight. Beatrice, trying to make sense of an intimate harbinger telling her that she was being targeted by unknown dark workings, remained guarded. She felt pushed towards the safety of the sunshine, and barely noticed Jake hanging on to her lips, waiting for her account of the secret meeting between Taylor and Doherty.

Beatrice felt suddenly pushed out of the boat, forced to swim with the small fry, gasping for air. Underneath the blanket of crass and odorous dead sea life, her heart fetl shackled to a destiny she didn't control. Meanwhile, she had to battle with the feeling that sharks were inevitable in the warm waters of vanity.

- 'She's the one, he said,' she rambled.
- 'Who said that?' blurted Jake, scrambling to find the pause button to his headphones, trying to decipher his friend's mumbling.
- 'I wonder what he meant by "she's the one",' she said.
- 'Who? Who said what?' Jake was panicked.

But Beatrice was walking vacantly towards an unknown future, her mouth gaping slightly, gasping, her face blushing with confusion and curiosity. They decided against queueing for the white orca and dolphin show, and headed for the Amusement park instead, as mosquitoes were incredibly voracious.

On the ride back to town and the amusement park, Beatrice remained tight-lipped, as if condemned to silence for a reason she could not explain.

- 'Something happened with Taylor, in the end, right?' asked Jake.
- 'How many times do I need to say it, nothing happened between me and Taylor, just let it go, will you? You are worse than my uncle!' she burst out with irritation.

She needed that silence. She was certain that Taylor and Doherty meant *she* was the one.
- 'What was he doing with Doherty at the aquarium, then?' Jake pressed her.

- 'I don't know … They just knew each other from Melbourne, I guess.
- You said "I wonder who the one is" back inside. What is wrong with you, Bee? You don't wanna tell me, fine!' said Jake, annoyed.

Among the rides of the amusement park, they met with two Japanese girls who were planning to go and ski in the North with their boyfriends. Beatrice needed an escape, away from Jake's relentless inquisition. She regained her composure at last:

- 'Wow, those noodles are so good! How do you say noodles in Japanese?' she asked to her new Japanese friend.

The flavours and aromas of the Japanese staple of scient mirin and vegetable broth opened her trepident mind to an immersive cultural experience.

- 'It depends whata kind offer noodale you mean,' said Haneko in English, in her thick Japanese accent. Haneko seemed to have been born with a frozen smile attached to her face. She was wearing a green cloche with a brim cap. In the queue to the giant roller-coaster, her sophisticated make-up had caught Beatrice's eye and the two girls had started a conversation. Jake was now looking for advice as to what food to eat.
- 'So what are these, then?' asked Jake.
- 'Ah! Chicken ramen!' said Haneko.
- 'So you say "chicken ramen" too in Japanese?' he asked, confused.

Haneko shook her head and signified "no" with a straight hand waving left and right. Jake looked at her body language, puzzled. She had raised a hand in front of her mouth, a polite idiosyncracy expressing shyness, humility and embarrassment at Jake's forthcomingness.

- 'Mine is soba!' exclaimed Jake. 'It says here in English. I'm ordering completely out of the blue.'
- 'Thank you for taking us and order for us,' said Beatrice, sympathetically. 'I wouldn't be able to even eat in this country if it wasn't for you. I have no idea what the menu says even though it's in English,' she chuckled.

The little noodle bar under the eye-in-the-sky attraction was packed with families and oddball office workers.

- 'I'd love to stay a bit longer in Yokohama,' said Beatrice, pouting her lips.
- 'Yeah, me too. There's so much to see and eat here,' said Jake, slurping his noodles noisily, imitating the bloke at the next table, who glanced at him sideways.

Haneko and Harua, the other Japanese girl, explained they wanted to take Beatrice and Jake for a night out. Towards the end of the afternoon, on the way to a karaoke bar, they also met two american boys, Jackson and Benjamin. Jackson was a student at the London Business school and his brother, a record producer from Michigan. The two Japanese girls' boyfriends, like two sneering black birds, tagged along nonchalantly, absorbed in their complicity. The six pack were now discussing what to do next …

- 'Jackson has an idea, girls! Why not try the overhead spinning coaster, but this time with these fellows, hey?' said Benjamin, a dark-haired male of Italian origin who meant to edge the group towards an orgy. He had taken a little bag of pills from his shirt pocket and was shaking it with a big grin.

Meanwhile, Jackson was being insistent with Beatrice. Jake came to her rescue. The hammy American duo were beginning to weigh on them.

- 'Typical control freak. What a pushy fella,' said Jake a few hours later, as they stepped into the lift of a close-by building where a restaurant with panoramic view was serving junk food, Japanese style: Western but healthy …
- 'Yeah … I just couldn't wait downstairs. I am not meddling with drugs, no way!
- Would your uncle kill you if you did?
- Unk? No!' said Beatrice, flushed because of the warm Japanese weather. 'He's open minded about these things, I think. I just don't want to lose my head over a few pills, that's all.

- I wish he'd told us more about his student days as a medical shrink, he must have had his own share of fun, right?'

They both giggled.

- 'I do like the idea of going back to the rides after dinner, though,' reflected Beatrice.
- 'Really? But, I thought you blew him off for good?' said Jake. Just teasing, really … He doesn't mean harm, he's just under my spell, I guess.'

The two Japanese girls had taken the lift ahead to find a table. Haneko was waiting for them by the "wait to be seated" sign.

- 'Do you see the American boys?' said Harua, a slim pretty girl who was wearing a tweed mini-skirt, high black boots, a bomber jacket and flashing jewellery.
- 'No, I didn't. We left them downstairs. We'll meet up again at the fair. Are you coming too?' asked Beatrice.
- 'Yes, my boyfriend loves rides.'

They sat down to a table under a gigantic aquarium filled with wondrous species. Jake was mesmerized by a large crab whose eyes were opening and closing like an automat. The two Japanese boys seemed overly quiet, pouring over the menu and groaning comments in Japanese to Haneko who seemed undecisive. Her head was tilted in a pondering pause. "Her blond hair clash with her jetdark eyebrows," thought Jake, while Beatrice and Harua conversed in broken English, bemused by the overhead aquarium teeming with eels.

- 'Still, Jake, those American boys reminded me of Taylor!'
- Yeah, spooky, right?'

The dinner table was lit up by a flashy neon sign, as an inside-out effect that Jake found mesmerizing. When the meal came to a close, all that was left on the table were empty plastic gobelets with colourful straws and empty chip bags, forlorn with satiated grease. The last slurps of rapacity fading out, Harua and

Beatrice decided to go back downstairs. Harua wanted to smoke. Jake meant to follow them, but Beatrice gestured for him to wait at the table:

- 'Girls like girls,' said one of the Japanese boys humorously, with a characteristic native tilt of the head, as Jake sat back down, hesitant and contradicted in his spontaneity. It was the first time one of them even spoke for that matter.
- 'Huh? No, she's straight … Oh, er … Gosh, I don't know.'
- You don't know?
- No, why?
- I don't know either, girls have many secrets, hey?' said Harua's boyfriend.

The Japanese boy put his finger across his mouth and laughed, commenting in Japanese to his friend, who nodded at his translation of the situation, and whose shaggy haircut intrigued Jake. Jake looked at Haneko who was fidgety. She rushed to pay the bill and walked towards the lift to meet the other girls downstairs. They all followed her in a whizz, and walked into the lift where one of the Japanese boys broke into a hip hop dance. The atmosphere became heated with eccentricity amid cocktail fizz. Jake was perplexed but amused. When they arrived on the ground floor, they met with the two girls who were waiting for the ascending lift. They all cheered each other in the cold and metallic lobby, and then naturally moved towards the exit, like a pod of dolphins hunting for mackerel, gregarious and fluid …But glancing back as he walked through revolving doors, Jake noticed two men sitting in the lounge downstairs. The silhouettes looked like cutouts against the neutral pastel décor, arranged as if to provide some intimacy to ghosts. He realised they were westerners watching them leave, as he followed the rest of the group towards the street. Jake thought he recognized Benjamin. The latter had given Jake a dark look and had immediately turned his head away. Next to him, Jake couldn't quite distinguish Jackson, his brother, but as he walked through the revolving doors, he had a sense of forewarning he hesitated to share with Beatrice for fear she might blank him out again. They then walked along the peer towards the lights and wonders of the amusement park, past a few posh hotels and the illuminated gardens of the sea-front Yamashita park, where statues of two children caught Beatrice's attention:

- 'Hey, who are those two girls statue in the park?' said Beatrice, inebriated by the cocktails she had knocked back like a fish.

Jake, tipsy, followed Beatrice as she waddled towards the statues. In the background, in a dry dock, a huge translatic steamer was laying still on the peer, against the dark horizon.

- 'Oh, it says here, "girl scouts … The friendship of something … "
- Ah, so, so so,' said Haneko excitedly. She pointed to the dry dock and the pacific steamer.
- 'Oh, I see, it's a historical thing, isn't it?'
- So, so, so. Transpacific. The first one,' answered Haneko keenly.

They both looked at the huge preserved transpacific steamer, a relic from the heydays of ferrycrossing.

- 'WWII stuff!' said Beatrice, holding an omniscient finger in the air, giggling.

The rest of the tribe were waiting by the sea side for the two girls, looking gleefully at the splashing water and the turbid swirls of the moonlit Pacific ocean swaying majestically beyond the safety rails. Jake looked back to see where Beatrice was at, when he noticed a man standing still, further up the peer, some fifty yards away. He thought he recognised Jackson's silhouette again …

- 'Beatrice?' shouted Jake, cupping his hands over his mouth.
- 'Whaaat?' she gestured back, wabbling awkwardly.
- 'Come here!' he signalled with a beckoning hand.

She raised her shoulders, palms facing upward. He saw her body now forming a weird W.
- 'What is it?' she gestured.

Walking back towards him reluctantly, she said:

- 'What is it now? Are you jealous of Haneko too?' she joked bleatingly.

- 'I think we are being followed,' said Jake.
- 'Followed?' Beatrice looked around, worried.
- 'Don't look, but back there, I think I recognised Jackson.
- Are you sure? Again? Where?
- I said "don't look". What part of "don't look" don't you get?'

She looked in the direction Jake was pointing to:

- 'Hey, Jackson, you coward!' hailed Beatrice.
- 'No! don't,' warned Jake. 'I think I also saw Benjamin downstairs at the restaurant tower, earlier.
- You're such a wolf-crier, aren't you,' Beatrice howled like a wolf.
- 'No! Bee, stop it! I think they were waiting for us. Maybe, they're not happy we gave them the slip, I don't know,' said Jake, trying to reason with her.

Jake became restless. Alerted by the worried expression on his face, Beatrice's hand swooshed in the air while she pampered her hair with the other:

- 'Oh, forget it!' Beatrice beaconed Haneko, who was still waiting by the sculptures like a dutiful schoolgirl.
- 'Ok, ayama cominga,' said the girl animatedly in her thick Japanese accent.
- 'Let's go, Jake. They won't try anything, there's too many of us,' said Beatrice, sobering up momentarily.

As they walked towards the fair, under the tall wharehouse buildings of the docks, their dwarfed silhouettes under the feeble lighting of the peer moved slowly towards Yokohama's fair, along more industrial and office buildings, and the sheer luminescence of the theme park. A few hundred yards down the peer, the six phantomatic figures carried on, unjolted by the Pacific violence of the dark opal ocean splashing against the embankment and its flaky handrails. The spray was cool and damp, and their banter and exchanges daring. But in the shadows, against the walls and behind the nooks of the architecture, an ominous shape was lurking menacingly, like a shark on the prowl …

Sat on a concrete block, outside the museum of science, Jonathan felt his spirit hover over Mount Tomurauchi where a thick mist, hanging over the flancs of the valley, prevented the sunlight from lighting his path. 'Find the mount, you'll find the monk,' he remembered Dubois's words, recollecting their phone conversation amidst a jetlag dip, soaking up the sunshine. They had arrived in Yokohama. The journey had been arduous but the reward was near ... Meanwhile, Dubois had been travelling up and down the country to find his friend, the raving monk, as he could not retrace the flower without him.

One cog he thought didn't quite fit in his symbolic journey towards the Everblue was Jake. He became aware of this undercurrent of thoughts, feeling its sinuous rivulets run wild and filter through the cracks of his conscience as he gawped at the artefacts of the Science museum display. The coastal city was the perfect place to lose Jake. *Who doesn't know how to use a camera?* he thought. Retrospectively, he could easily justifiy the whole case of his disappearance as a necessary milestone towards the Everblue. After all, expeditions had collaterals. The astronaut suit in the space travel section, once wore by the first Japanese space-hopper, seemed to concur.

Jake was becoming a nuisance. He was already showing signs of overstepping boundaries, making sardonic comments about Jonathan's every move, undermining his authority. Little by little, he could threaten to dishearten Beatrice, who would eventually take a flight back home or travel to the South and the hot weather. She would be snatched by young people her age and would soon forget about their expedition. Who knew which of her teen spirit or her dutiful mind would win this battle of wills? It was quite possible they would both change their mind, a typical passtime at their age. Their fake sibling love felt suddenly repulsive to Jonathan ... Beatrice had already been in a fit of the sulks at the idea of journeying in the cold mountains of the North of Japan. Now that he had no other choice but to explore the city on his own. Since Jake and Beatrice had rather visited Yokohama's amusement park, it all became clear what had to happen.

His shadowy thoughts lingered on until the forensic science display, where the real smell of blood and iron made his stomach retch. The throng of children rushing towards the themed restaurant where people were queuing for some interactive organoleptic games awakened his empathy. It was time to start exploring his pulsions towards Beatrice, as his antagonism towards Jake scared him. What was overtaking him suddenly? Were his murderous impulse due to the ever closer proximity of the Everblue?

February in Japan was mild and pleasant. Most of the locals were already boasting about the imminent blooming season, which, according to the sparkling eyes of the bloom watchers and the media frenzy spurring them on, could not be missed. Jonathan had to keep his eyes on the prize. The *piece de resistance* couldn't wait. Beatrice and him had travelled too far together.

Little Death

Catherine was a fake Bohemian, nothing short of a calculated lunatic and a venal romantic, according to Roger Doherty, the self-proclaimed spiritualist, who thought it timely to educate Jonathan about the spirituality of the ancient Aztecs at the Dakuza family pension, providing examples of their beliefs to better highlight the case of the Everblue and the impact of its discoveries for the aspiring human race:

- 'You can't just dump such a discovery on the people of the old world without some sort of explanation, a framework, or at least a proven model that works for everyone!' humoured Jonathan in the lounge of the small Japanese guest house where Dubois had arranged for a series of rooms on the same floor. The debate had started on the third floor and continued throughout breakfast, here in Shirataka. Jonathan had not minded so much Doherty's description of his aunt, which he thought was accurate, but Doherty's sandalled flippancy exacerbated his jetlag hangover.
- 'Oh, don't take it personally, Mr. Doherty, he's been in that mood since we left Scotland,' said Beatrice, laying down her handbag on one of the lounge sofas, as she entered the sober Japanese interior of the breakfast area.

Doherty, Jake, Beatrice and Jonathan were Indian sitting in their socks though breakfast at the neatly organised row of low cherry wood tables, surrounded by pine wood panels. Past the introductions and the good spirited jellied eels, miso soup broth and pancaked eggs, men indulged in shoptalk squabbling, exchanging quid pro quos over the Japanese feast.

- 'Unless you change models in Society, you can't introduce such a discovery as the Everblue! It's the norms that are the cause of most mental health issues anyway, as shown by the study carried out by the National Institute,' retorted Doherty, still harebrained on the age-old chicken and egg argument.
- 'And what National Institute is that, the Bonkers bikers? Don't forget to wear your helmet, Doherty!
- That's a bit thick, coming from flesh-hunting hustlers and drug-pushers like yourselves, working from government guidelines that foster incomprehension! You can't see the wood for the trees, seeking to profit from mental health and milk the health budget!
- Banking on spiritual needs to make a quick buck is better, is it?' argued Jonathan offhandedly, now that his argumentative verve had elapsed.
- 'There aren't any trees left in our country anyway!' shouted Jake, suddenly agitated by their heated conversation, seeking undue attention. 'I mean can't you two at least agree on something, collude or whatever it's called?
- Collude?' asked Doherty, disgruntled and indignant.
- 'Yes, Jake, whatever do you mean?' said Jonathan on a derisive tone.
- 'I mean, get on, work together!' said Jake, sheepishly.
- 'Oh, psychoanalysis can't do anything for the world, I am afraid,' groaned Doherty, brushing off Jake's remark.
- 'Resolutely over-misoed,' said Beatrice, shaking her head at Jake, referring to her salty soybean broth.
- 'As if spirituality could do anything against the reality of death, grow up, Doherty, you have to call a slab a slab!' said Jonathan.

Beatrice explained she meant to do a bit of shopping all morning in the medieval Japanese market, where small huts had been converted into tourist shops. She tied her long blond hair in a pony tail and kissed Jonathan and Jake on the cheek.

- 'Quack!' said Jonathan, between his teeth, offering his cheek to Beatrice.

Dubois was due to make an appearance later that day, with news from his friend, the raving monk. Jake felt suddenly crippled without the comfort of Beatrice's presence, despairingly looking at the two men, his fist clenched behind the Dakuza communal couch, as Beatrice left the breakfast lounge. Jake ultimately found himself in the company of Jonathan against his will. As Doherty had himself stormed off back to his quarters, Jake was determined to learn more about the psychiatrist's journey.

- 'You're a psychiatrist, Jonathan, right? Do you always analyse people or is it just work?' said Jake, genially.
- 'Don't you have some interests of your own, boy?' said Jonathan, falsely congenial.

He meant to nip the young man's attempt at a leisurely talk in the bud. Jake looked suspiciously at Jonathan's hot smouldering black coffee.

- 'We saw Doherty and Taylor at the aquarium. It looked as if they knew each other,' said Jake on a confidential tone.
- 'Who's Taylor?' asked Jonathan distractedly.
- 'The American boy we met in Melbourne.
- Oh, yes. And?
- It's just weird. I thought I heard Beatrice say that they were conspiring,' said Jake.

Jonathan chuckled loudly:

- 'Conspiring? About what?
- I dunno, don't you find it weird?' said Jake.
- 'Didn't Beatrice say Taylor was coming to Japan? They must have met by chance … Doherty at the aquarium? How interesting.
- Beatrice heard them talk and she was quite disturbed afterwards.
- What do you mean, disturbed?
- She didn't wanna talk about it!
- She probably thought it was too much of a conspiracy theory,' said Jonathan.

Jake saw a dark twinkling in Jonathan's eyes that told him he'd better change the subject.

- 'Anyway … I was wondering about what you do with people like me, if you have them as client,' said Jake.
- What do you mean, people like you?
- 'I am autistic, I've been told … I mean, I'm doing fine, but as a student,
- I kinda struggle to find my way through the normal education system.'

Jake used his fingers to bracket the word "normal".

- 'Ah, ok, well, autism is not a mental health issue as such, so I don't see what I could do for you,' said Jonathan.
- 'But …Listen, Jake … I am retired, and besides, do you really fancy the role of the guinea pig? If your answer is "yes" to that question, then, you might as well talk to Doherty about it. I mean, am I the only one to see how important this expedition is? Can't anyone see the magnitude of the discovery of the Everblue?' roared Jonathan.

He had lost his temper before, in the minivan, on the way to Sidney, recalled Jake. He had the T-shirt: Jonathan was famously and bitterly unpredictable of late.

- 'I know my place, Mr. Deadstone, I am only here to take photographs. You said it so yourself.
- Your mind may be grumbled at times, but you're not mentally-ill, Jake,' reasoned Jonathan, placid.
- 'I just meant to ask you about your job. Maybe, you don't feel like talking about it, that's fine. I'll just take a few pictures until Beatrice comes back from her shopping, then.
- Yes, Jake, sounds like a plan. And I have things to discuss with Dubois, but I am always available to talk about your issues, if you want.
- Sure, yeah. You bet!'

Jake felt discombobulated by Jonathan's typical parental reaction, but put it down to the generational gap between them. After all, as a friend of Beatrice, he only meant to show respect for her uncle by letting him in the loop. He felt saddened that Jonathan refused his attempt at making a show of humility. Far from him the idea of bonding with a cantankerous shrink, he had simply meant to break the ice.

During the day, Jake photographed the Japanese countryside and its native tree species: the sakura cherries of course, with their shiny layered bark, and the colourful maples, proudly bearing the next season's fruitfulness on their branches, budding in many ways into his imagination as visible signs of youthfulness. Jake, still jet-lagged, struggling with the intensity of daylight, realised he had been treated unfairly, but that somehow, Jonathan was justified in feeling that way towards him because he was seen as a threat to his unique relationship with Beatrice. It was obvious to Jake that Jonathan saw him as a competitor.

When Beatrice returned from her rampage on the touristic shops in Shirataka, she called Jake whose photographic journey had taken him too far in the countryside. He had tried to call her because he had gotten lost and was standing in front of a shrine below a sitka spruce, between two stone lanterns.

- 'Oh my God! What are you doing there, Jake?' said Beatrice at the other end.
- 'I dunno, I just walked out of town and here I am!
- Can't you ask someone? I'm still shopping, they'll tell you where you are, surely?
- What, but I don't speak Japanese!
- Speak English then!
- But there's no one around!
- Walk back to where you come from, then!
- If I knew that, I wouldn't be calling you, would I?
- Have you used Google maps?
- Huh? Oh, yeah, I see what you mean, let me call you back.'

Vying for attention in the best way he could, Jake found an old Japanese tractor that took him back to the edge of town. The kind farmer was dressed in a strangely clean blue working suit that looked like a uniform. He smiled at him all the way back to town, nodding his head, although he had no idea what Jake was trying to say. His buried face was tanned and his smiling eyes barely visible underneath his bushy eyebrows. Googling his way back home was easier with street names and a Wifi connection. Before long, Jake was sitting in the lounge, feeling sorry for his absent-mindedness, but eager to share his photographic work with Beatrice or anyone who would be interested.

- 'So Dubois didn't come?' said Beatrice, who was wearing a purple see-through sarong.
- 'No, I dunno. Nice saran, you have,' said Jake, back at the Dakuza guest-house, sitting on a large boulder in the neat courtyard, where a Koy fish pond had inspired his artistic self.
- Saran? As in Saran wrap? Thank you, Jake, but I am wearing a Sarong, it's a Malay word for a loose garment wore leisurely by women of taste,' said Beatrice, exaggeratingly standoffish, twirling coquettishly, like a model.
- 'Is your uncle in?' said Jake, suddenly sombre.
- 'Why?' said Beatrice, interrupting her little girl's impersonation.
- 'We had a chat before you left and I am afraid I might have made him angry.
- You can't make anyone angry, don't worry. You're such a nice fellow, Jake. Everyone adores you!' she said, resuming her princess act.
- 'Please, don't make fun of me, Bee.'

Jake's expression changed from consternation to excitement as he showed Beatrice his pictures of the day.

- 'Cool! It pays getting lost sometimes, don't you think?
- Yeah ... I came home in a tractor! The farmer looked at me and kept saying "Yakushi, Yakushi." I wish I knew what that meant.'

They both laughed, resuming their innocent banter. Dubois was a man with a mission. He had managed to convince half a dozen of people that a flower could change the world. But here he was, at Shirataka station, in a small wood cabin surrounded by misty luxurious hills looking at a deserted station, surveying the landscape and the illisible signs around him. A train attendant spotted the short sturdy foreigner. Jonathan's pre-cognitive dream had been realised.

However, Dubois wouldn't be flanked by a monk but a Japanese train official in full uniform who, try as he might, couldn't string two words of English together.

- 'Yakuza! Yakuza!' kept repeating Dubois.

The Japanese train official was beating his chest in disbelief.

- 'Watashi, no! Not Yakuza!
- But the hotel is called Yakuza, not you!' said Dubois, who understood "Watashi" meant "I"
- 'Takshi? Takshi? Hotelu?' said the Japanese trainman.
- 'Yes, please, hotelu,' conceded Dubois.
- 'Adressu?' said the train attendant.
- 'No, janai.' said Dubois, meaning he had lost the address of the family guest-house.

A taxi wouldn't quite solve the matter for Dubois, who all polite smiles considered realised "Yakuza" could also describe a member of the organised crime syndicates. A taxi was called nevertheless while he collected his thoughts.

- 'It can't be Yakuza,' whimpered Dubois, sitting on the rear seat of a cab, fumbling for the little paper note he had scribbled with the name of the Dakuza guest house's address. Why on earth would anyone call a private pension "Yakuza", he wondered, padding a carton file folder, worried it might have gotten damp in the morning mist.

The taxi took him to a fashion shop as soon as he said the word "Yakuza". From then, it took him the whole morning to find the guest-house. As soon as he arrived at the address that, unfortunately, he had mistakenly mispelt on a loose piece of paper, he began worrying he might have arranged for a hotel that his guests would never find. Fortunately, he did have the phone number and before his Japanese experience in town turned into a quid pro quo as to whether he was looking for gansters in this small, rural mountain side town, he called the hotel and finally talked to Jonathan who received a call from a female shop attendant and understood that Dubois had finally made it on planet Japan. He met with Dubois some time later at a family mart, where a young Japanese shop assistant had kindly taken him under her wing. The two men were soon walking alongside a river …

- 'But you know,' said Dubois, walking by Jonathan's side, 'the hotel wasn't called Yakuza at all. It's just that I had noted it that way.
- Mistakes happen, Charles. And we're all here, after all. The Dakuza is a charming place. I met with Doherty, and I am afraid I must be frank. I don't really see what he's doing here, apart from peacocking as would-be guru.
- Well, maybe you should hold your disbelief back a bit, Jonathan. He's a good friend of Catherine's, bless her soul, and he could be useful. Bless your friend as well, I am sorry he died.
- My friend?
- Well, he died, didn't he?' said Dubois.
- 'Not at all, do you mean, Charles, my monkey?
- Oh, sorry. There again, you see, my memory is strangely confused these days.
- He was a friend, after all,' pondered Jonathan.
- 'Oh, yes, whether it's because I'd blocked out his death as inconceivable because we share the same name, I don't know, but it's yet another stupid mistake I made.
- Not at all, mistakes happen, Charles.'

Jonathan fell suddenly silent, realising that he had taken a couple of young people out here in a completely isolated part of a foreign country where he couldn't speak the language, only to string them along with an anthropologist with onset dementia and whose only friend was a raving monk. He did wonder why they were all here miles away from Tomurauchi mount where the flower was effectively supposed to have been, but the jet-lag thought process was too much to handle bar a good lunch.

- 'Still, I have made progress! The monk's name was not his official identity, as you can imagine. But I found his records from the temple he used to officiate at,' said Dubois.
- 'Good, now that's a start. But why are we here?' asked Jonathan.

- 'Well, as I explained in my letter, the same flower has been spotted here and there can be no ambiguity. The same story from a different monk, who doesn't travel by modern means has been told to me again in the same precocious details. He will come later, Jonathan. God knows when, I'm afraid.
- Yes, I understood that, Charles. And I'm grateful for your trust in the matter. I suppose Doherty's presence is still a bone of contention in my mind. Nevertheless, that flower seems a bit too ubiquitous to me.
- No doubt, you two have a lot to smooth over, but the spiritual side of the matter is essential here!' said Dubois with pusillanimity.
- 'Talking about spirituality, Charles, did you spot the flower yourself, have you seen it? Why such a mystery around its location now that we're all here?'

Dubois wagged the flat of his hand to tell Jonathan to slow down.

- 'In time, Jonathan, all in good time.'

Dubois wanted to walk back into the family mart so he could buy a plug adaptor. Jonathan was told to wait outside. He surmised that Dubois had triaged the participants according to their skills. But did that mean that he was there to ensure all members of this new Everblue sect stayed whole? Emotional reality aside, what could he possibly do against magic, if it came to that, let alone sorcery? But Dubois came out of the store in the middle of his introspective meditation.

- 'If I am being honest, Jonathan, I have been having lucid dreams about my death.
- Oh … Death hey? What about your adaptor?'

Jonathan stopped the sturdy old man in his energetic walk, holding him back.

- 'Oh, they haven't got any,' said Dubois, who seemed to be throwing an imaginary towel behind his shoulders.
- 'Damn … It sucks. No phone then, hey, Charles?'

Jonathan's mind had travelled to Beatrice and his lasting grief since Eleanor's death. He meant to say bluntly "Charles? Can your death wait till after lunch?" but refrained.

- 'Charles … There's more to life than death. I am sure we should have a wonderful lunch and then, we can discuss your dreams. But in my experience, a heavy dinner is always followed by vivid dreams. Do you usually have heavy diners, Charles?
- Still, I have been facing my own death and it's been weighing on my mind. I was wondering if I could run it by you after lunch,' said Dubois, visibly absorbed by his own thoughts.

They had sushi onigiri, small balls of rice topped with raw fish slices and prawn gyoza, a fine dumpling skin wrapper served with a sweet sticky sauce in a small local restaurant, along Shirataka's market street. Dubois complimented the chef on the quality of his deserts in his stilted Japanese. It was the best "Paris-Best" he had ever tasted. After lunch, Jonathan walked Charles to a local park to hear his version of Dubois' dream about his own death.

- 'I had foreseen that my presence might be needed because of my experience and skills, but I had hoped I would avoid practising al fresco,' Jonathan joked. Dubois sniggered.
- 'Ah, I must have been working too hard,' said Dubois, sitting down smacking his thighs with both hands.

In a small park where they found a wooden bench surrounded by azaleas, they watched in the distance a little boy playing under the loose supervision of his reading mother.

- 'My dream is the following: I am lying on a huge stone, it is pouring down with rain and I can see myself lying there, as in an out of body experience,' said Dubois.
- 'Carry on …That's it!
- And how do you wake up from that dream?' asked Jonathan.
- 'Of course …I mean how do you feel when you wake up?
- I am sweating, I guess …I mean, how do you actually feel?

- Rested too, but somehow, struggling … to feel it's not real,' said Dubois.
- 'I think you just suffer from the high level of humidity and you might also have some anxiety about your legacy. What you describe is the funeral pyre of Celtic kings, I believe. You're obviously afraid that something might happen to you during this expedition, but you are also eager to see it through. The rain and the stone are symbolic of the passage of time and the wear and tear of the ages. That boulder is a milestone, as far as I can make it. I could check up your vitals if you didn't have a check-up before you travelled. I would be happy to auscult you … Better safe than sorry. The stone slab is more of a preoccupation than a symptom of anything existential, really. You wonder whether you will die here, but wouldn't that be a great end to a heroic story, Charles?' said Jonathan.
- 'Well, I … I don't quite see myself dying just now. Maybe, now you mention it. I might have some of the martyr king in me.
- Yes, I think that it's both a preoccupation and a fantasy, which obviously is conflicting,' said Jonathan.
- 'Ah … I had not seen it that way,' said Dubois, perplex.
- 'Animistic fantasies are common, you know … You may be influenced by what Jung called the "unconscious collective".'
- The "unconscious collective", how?
- 'Your subconscious is not entirely yours to experience … You picture your death as an animistic fatality. Over here, where the structures of society are utterly different, you compensate for the lack of Christian structure with a heroic death scenario … But I am not a Christian, but an atheist!
- Nevertheless, you were born and raised within its conceptual structures. Besides, whatever you saw or heard while being here may have connected to your own personal fantasy world. Without going into details, because of your cultural immersion, you are part of a whole that dreams during the night and is culturally active during the day. Your ancestral past is somewhere out there, available to tap into but is not the same as these people's ancestral past. Imagine your subconscious as a substation being part of a wider network. Being here is a whole new setting for your brain to work out, but distance with your body could also be a great revealer of a deeper trauma too. Do you have children?

- I have two, and they're all grown up now,' said Dubois, suddenly nostalgic.
- 'Boys or girls?
- Two girls … I will tell you more later, but … It remains, you are thinking of them as you think of your own legacy, and well-being of course. Your out of body experience is interesting. We might need to probe that further.
- In what way, may I ask? You've said some intriguing things,' said Dubois.
- 'We night look at the clothes you wear in your dreams for example, but you might only remember the details under hypnosis. At this stage, we should leave it there. Jetlag is a strong trigger. I can't walk and hypnotise like lawyers do,' said Jonathan.

Dubois smiled. Jonathan felt the expedition was becoming clearer in his mind, but he himself smiled for other reasons. He was looking forward to seeing Beatrice's new clothes, for instance. Simple details like these were often on his mind, lately. Later in the afternoon, Jonathan greeted Beatrice as soon as he heard her steps in the corridor:

- 'Did you have a nice time, darling?
- Hi, Unk! Yes, apart from Jake getting lost in the countryside, I told him to Google map it, but he didn't have Wi-Fi, he was okay in the end, though.
- Oh, now you realise what you were getting into, hey?
- What do you mean?' said Beatrice, her face frozen her mouth wide-open in disingenuous indignation.
- 'I mean, sorry. I feel sorry for him, that's all. We all do.
- Oh, yes, well, don't be. Listen, I need a warm bath.'

Jonathan suddenly felt excited at the idea of Beatrice visting him in her bathrobe, after her bath.

- 'I think a massage would do you good.
- You don't want to come across as a perv, Unk, now do you?'

Jonathan chuckled with her in unison, but couldn't not grab the opportunity.

- 'Not, if you don't want me to.
- Ballsy! Come on, Unk, what's between me and you is already challenging as it is …But, Beatrice … It doesn't have to be,' said Jonathan, edging closer to her bedroom door, smoothing his masculine voice with one of his most caring unctuous tone.
- 'I really need a shower, Unk. If you want, I can come and see you later. Sometimes, it's what we want for ourselves that we won't do to others.
- That's a brilliant idea!' said Jonathan, beaming.

Jonathan rode waves of joy all evening, even after the diner with Doherty. He couldn't understand what he had meant by "That's a brilliant idea" but beamed all the same. After all, this pussy-footing would not just bring them closer, but would definitely intensify any sexual tension. If only she would acclimatise to the idea that he could take care of her body, then, he would see if the connection he felt were to remain in the realm of fantasy or not. *Fantasy is a wonderful thing*, thought Jonathan. The joy he felt at Beatrice's willingness to explore quenched his curiosity for the time being, but for how long? She said: 'Sometimes, it's what we want for ourselves that we won't do to others'. What did she mean by that. Surely, it meant that she was expectant on him to probe further his fantasy. He relied on Beatrice to show maturity in that regard, as he would help her journeying towards the Everblue. He didn't sleep that night. The day had been hot and the sheer munificence of her young age on the altar of love aroused a desire that he hadn't felt in the flesh for a long time. It's not so much his objectification of her that he had trouble disentangling from, as his masculine urges needed no schooling, but the precious bond they had built after her father's death, which remained a road block. He embarked on the journey through the fatherly feelings that he nurtured towards her, but only to realise that it would serve his desire better if he let her shepperd his lust. How diverse and exhausting those scenarios were was the reason he wasn't sleeping. He felt tempted to go and visit her to open his heart. But it was too soon …

Initiation

The milky way over Hokkaido … An open gash in the vault of the sky. A blue and white jaspé halo of speckled luminous stars. The immense and bountiful bareness of the harsh, cruel, salient rocks. The dwarfing pull and push of the ravines' dark groaning and cracking … A shredded mist was hanging over the surrounding mountain tops, anchored into knolls and crevices like Deadman's fingers. The variegated shadows of a ghostly presence kissing the curves, twists and swells of the mountain flanks, the sheer magnificence of the valleys and slopes awash with the anticipation of light. In the distance, over the camp, the Safran horizon soon teemed with warm sun rays bursting through the dark veil of the night …

- 'It was too soon, wasn't it?
- What was too soon, who's this?' It was Dubois' head voice. Jonathan heard it distinctly.
- 'Your initiation to the Everblue …
- Is that you Charles?
- This is Master Khul, isn't it?'

Voices gelled in the silence of dawn, reverberating in Dubois's subconscious as he turned over on his side. Under his sleeping bag and a thick blanket of wool, his mind was the theater of a universal awakening. It seemed that Dubois's spirit was wandering to the top of the Tomurauchi mountain once again. As the magical influence of the Everblue blurred the boundaries between life and death, between omniscience and nothingness, Dubois unknowingly started conversing with his after-life spirit as Jonathan was privy to his thoughts. Dubois' subconscious suddenly exposed, Jonathan, at a few tents' distance, shirked at first. His whole body trembling with resistance. A case of telepathy.

Here, on the rocky plateau, mid-way to the top of Mount Asahi, all was quiet. There was no doubt. The epicenter of Dubois's awakening, where the universe had entered his soul, was suddenly felt by Jonathan like a human emergency.

- 'What was his name?
- His name?
- Your friend, the monk … What was his name?
- Who's speaking? Is that you, Deadstone?'

The terrible power of the flower, he could see it now, blurring the boundaries between fantasy and reality, a blue and radiant metaphysical wonder, as bright as the North Star, the star of travellers.

- 'His name was Khul.
- Why was it too soon, Charles?'

Dubois's lips were moving in his sleep, his whole body petrified with awe.

- 'I can't re … member his face,' Dubois' lips babbled.

Jonathan was barely awake, listening to Dubois's mind-voice despite his qualms. He kept his eyes shut in his tent, at the bottom of Mount Asahi, a few yards from Dubois'. Jonathan kept an open mind, for fear of dispelling a once-in-a-lifetime hallucination. He knew his spirit would be travelling back to the Tomurauchi mountain and the phantomatic village along with Dubois'. A telepathetic communication between the two had been initiated by a blackhole, overtaking their consciousness. Jonathan suddenly became aware of his own dream flow as he heard Dubois' voice enter his consciousness.

- 'Master Khul says to look on the other side of the mountain. It is always hidden on the north-facing slope, away from view,' said Dubois.

A timeless telepathic conversation, a flash of universal knowledge, as if it came from the immensity of the milky way, their soul stretching to reach the vault of eternal knowledge. When dream spirits meet, there is only illusion:

- 'Here were are, Charles,' said Jonathan, steadfast in his dreaming state.
- 'Is that Jonathan Deadstone?
- Yes.
- I am here with Master Khul, once more, Jonathan.
- Aye.
- It's time he told you that no man is mad. Here it is, the spirit of the flower, take it …Aye.
- It's here with us …Now I see,' answered Jonathan.

Their voices were dubbed, toneless and floating, as if sensed, not heard. Dubois could now distinctly see Master Khul's face as the monk meditated profoundly on a sack of cloth in one of the abandoned shacks; a tea set made of forged iron laid at his feet, in the middle of the room. The candles, burning, the wax, melting … His legs in the lotus position, his hands anchored to his knees, gravitatiomnally free, hollow, like a hologram with indefinite layers of nothing. His face bathing in an aura that he felt both frightening and hypnotic. The concrete world floating around them, their diluted spirit blended in an enveloppe of light. Dubois struggled to breathe. He felt the need to rush to Jonathan's tent and talk to him face to face, but couldn't move.

- 'It's time, Charles, your dream will be realised soon,' said Jonathan's voice.
- 'The Everblue is near … ' Dubois's last sigh closed their share waking dream.

Into the silence of the night, Mount Asahi's dark revelation retreated before the radiant light of the morning. Jonathan opened his eyes: he felt all the vicissitudes of life he had tamed in his body, soul and mind, arrested, suspended in the illusory world of mind-matter. Jonathan tried to remember the name he had heard during his sleep. It was Cool … Master Cool? He hanged on to the sound he had heard, but felt it slip away, before the wakefulness of nature around him engulfed its shredded remnants. The squawking of a moutain-hawk eagle, the sound of the wind, the rustle of sleeping bodies in the tents awoke him to his own reality. He saw the roof of his tent, the colour of the canvass now crudely clear. He closed his eyes once more to try and carve the name of the Master in his mind. "Master Cool, was it not?"

Jonathan was the first to get up in the camp, among the tents gathered in a semi-circle, Jake's at the very end, next to Jonathan's, to Beatrice's, to Doherty's and to Dubois'. He put on his trousers and shoes and walked towards Dubois's tent. All were still asleep. As he opened the zip of Dubois' tent, he had a pre-cognitive feeling that death was there. He shook Dubois gently, called out his name. Since he wasn't answering, he shook Dubois's body harder before taking his pulse. Dubois had died but a few minutes ago.

His own body suddenly felt hollow, emptied of meaning ... He lay down Dubois's head with solemnity. For a few stealthy seconds, he felt the whole gravity of death dragging his soul back to the dream he had shared with Dubois. He waited for the familiar passing feeling of guilt mixed with powerlessness, relief and sorrowful exultation he had felt many times during his medical career to blow over. The morning cold and the mist down the valley helped him recollect his thoughts for a brief moment before he felt the vigour of life circulating around his body again. His own heart was beating for sure. The feeling of empathy for Dubois lying there inside the sleeping bag and the tent had naturally overwhelmed him. He thought of his last words and the dream, but found only shreds of it, overblown by fear and controlled anger. It was too soon to form a picture of the man in his wholeness yet, or how he had felt the entireity of his soul during their telepathic dream. So Jonathan searched for an explanation for this sudden insight. He had felt it during a split second and it had filled him with the spirit of a dying man. It was unlike what he had ever felt before as a medical doctor. Patients died ... Dubois was no exception, but he had been pretold of this death by the very man he was looking at. He remembered his conversation a few days before. He stepped away from the tent quietly and took a deep breath, a chill running through his body still, as he fumbled for Dubois's Dunhill in his coat pocket and took a cigarette out of the box. A mechanic gesture. He lit it up and inhaled the smoke, coughed a little. A casual smoker's cough. His light blue eyes then surveyed the ochre valley where the mist still hanged like a shredded veil over the face of rocks. He watched the spectacle of the morning changing hues and the shadow of passing clouds being ushered along by the winds. He saw the mountain turn from yellowish grey to ochre and then from ochre to orange. The sun soon illuminated the East face where sun pillars were forming in the valley.

He looked down below searching for a slab that matched Dubois's dream ... As he suspected, it was right there, a few yards down the slope, big enough for his strapping body, shining with diamond dust, exposed before his eyes as the concrete irremediable realisation of his passing. He decided there and then that Dubois's vision should be staged as he had described it.

Beatrice was the first being he saw alive. Until now, he had felt in between the two waters of sleep and death, looking at the precipice below, smoking one of Dubois's cigarettes:

- 'Morning Unk. Do you smoke now? Shall we move today? I might need more than a sleeping bag as last night was freezing, I swear!' said Beatrice. He looked at her, haggard.

He acknowledged her candidness with a constricted smile. She ruffled her hair with her fingers, yawning, her eyes puffed up with sleep.

- 'Did you have sweet dreams, darling?' he said.
- 'The feeling of the sky above is fantastic, but the mountain is far from quiet. Did you hear that huge crashing sound in the night?
- Yes, it woke me up. Stones probably. It sounded like a landslide. The snow is thawing on the peaks, I guess … What is it, Unk? You look pale?
- Dubois's dead,' he said in a matter-of-fact way.
- 'What???
- He died this morning. He called me … He called you, how?
- Oh, you know, he called me.
- Oh,' said Beatrice, unsure of what Jonathan meant. 'What are we gonna do?' she exclaimed suddenly, her palms against her cheeks, a discomfit air passing over her subdued mien.
- 'Dubois must have left instructions. The monk he was waiting for should join us later today, I think,' said Jonathan, calmly.
- 'I mean with his body?'

Beatrice hesitated before rushing to Jake's tent. Jonathan watched her tiptoeing away. Before calling for emergency services to take the body away, Jonathan later insisted a ceremony should be held. Doherty, who emerged from his tent upon hearing voices joined Jonathan in front of the departed's. He raised his eyebrows at the news:

- 'Before going further, what makes you think this is what he wanted?' Doherty argued, outraged, his face red with both indignation and the morning cold.
- 'He told me about his dream outside the family mart in town. He told me he'd seen his death in his dreams. I know it sounds unorthodox, but that's how he wanted it,' said Jonathan, resigned.
- 'What did he die of?' asked Doherty, dubitative.
- 'His heart gave in I think. But I would need a history to tell you more.
- But did he leave any special instructions?' said Doherty, panicking.
- 'Only a telepathic conversation we had just before his last breath.
- Oh, Lord … ' said Doherty, rolling his eyes.
- 'So what, past you 5–9 spiritualism, you're lost, is that it? Will you help me or what? There's a slab down below, over there!' said Jonathan.
- 'What? No way!' said Doherty, horrified.

He showed Doherty the stone slab hanging over the precipice of a cliff, overlooking the valley.

- 'And? What next?' groaned Doherty.
- 'We'll just lay his body down there until the ambulance helicopter arrives. Meanwhile, I'll check his personal effects to see if he left any written instructions.
- Is this some kind of Hindu ceremony?' asked Doherty, puzzled.
- 'No, Celtic I imagine. Dubois was French, from Britanny.'

Doherty finally came round to the idea, albeit with much effort on Jonathan's part. They finally motioned to carry the body away. Jake and Beatrice could be heard whispering in Jake's tent. Jonathan and Doherty were about to remove the body from Dubois's tent when they heard footsteps coming from the trail. They both watched the bowing head of a mountaineer bobbing under a wooly cap. The beaming smile of the man left Jonathan bemused for a minute, as he was holding Dubois by the armpits. Doherty rushed to meet the stranger, namasteing the monk as if he were a hindu messiah, dropping Duibois' legs in the process.

- 'Yoroshiku gozaimasu!' said the monk, introducing himself, bowing low.

Jonathan laid Dubois's body down.

- 'Pleased to meet you,' said Jonathan, bowing too.
- 'Mister Dubois?' enquired the monk, pointing at Dubois's tent.
- 'Yes. He's dead, I'm afraid,' said Jonathan.

He explained to the monk that Dubois had had a dream just before his death and that he and Doherty intended to honour his last wishes.

- 'I will bless,' said the monk.
- 'Master Hashita, is Master Cool with you?' asked Doherty.

The monk shook his head calmly.

- 'I'll be dammed,' said Doherty, 'we're fucked!'
- 'What do you mean, "fucked"?', asked the monk, visibly lost in translation.
- 'Sorry, I am just thinking out loud,' apologized Doherty.
- 'Thinking out loud, no good. Silence good,' said the monk.
- 'Yes, I agree. For now, let's move Dubois. I will call the ambulance next, we'll see later what the future has in store for us with the help of Master Hashita,' said Jonathan decisively.
- 'You still want the Everblue, right?' said the monk.
- 'Yes,' said Jonathan. 'But not today, as you can see.'

The monk sidestepped to let them pass, and proceeded to unpack his tent which he installed next to Dubois'. The latter's body was carried down the rocky and slippery rocks towards a large stone slab hanging over the precipice. The two men then covered it with Dubois' tent canvass and weighed it down with rocks. Beatrice, Doherty and Jake were put in charge of gathering stones to make a makeshift sepulchre.

- 'We should be able to build a rampart with stones too, I don't wanna be accused of feeding a corpse to scavengers, last wishes or no last wishes!' said Doherty, enervatedly.
- 'Of course, Roger,' Beatrice reassured him patronizingly.

Doherty mulled over his dismal task dolefully.

- 'Roger, may I ask you something?' asked Jake tentatively.
- 'Sure, buddy,' answered Doherty, pleased to see they were showing interest. 'What is the future made of?
- Right. Well, the present is made of dreams. The future is forgetful and the past, an eternal question. We'd better gather as many stones as we can before the storm, children,' said Doherty, puffing.

Jake and Beatrice stayed behind, in their little impromptu quary, while Doherty carried stones back to the camp in his rucksack.

- 'Bee, I don't want to pry but is Jonathan in love with you?' asked Jake out of the blue, raising his head from his labour.

Beatrice looked at him from the corner of her eye. She took a deep breath and sighed.

- 'Is it so obvious, Jake?
- And do your love him? Be honest,' asked Jake, daring her.
- 'I do. He's my uncle.
- You know what I mean … Jake, stop it! You're prying. You said you didn't want to pry and yet, you're prying now.
- I am sorry, Bee … It's just that you let him in.
- I don't get to choose whether I let him in or not. When you're in love, you'll understand.
- Okay, I'll try to remember,' said Jake.

They didn't look at each other until enough stones were gathered. Their conversation went on as they picked up rocks to build a hearth against the elements as instructed by Jonathan who had decided to make a tower some four of five foot tall, big enough to protect the men from the brewing storm, around the life-essential fire. Beatrice stood up, watching Jake picking up a pebble, admiring it, as if it were a work of art.

- 'It's funny how these beach pebbles found themselves on a mountain,' said Jake, musingly.
- 'Jake … Let's bring back those stones and go back down to find a hotel, shall we?' said Beatrice.
- 'Yeah, agreed! Let's get out of here!' said Jake, jubilant. 'Tonight's going to be fun,' he said, now lying on the heather as it was a pouch, holding the stone in his hand behind his head.'

Doherty returned with an empty rucksack. He dropped it at the foot of their pile, panting for breath:

- 'Well, this is our last trip. What have you two been up to?' said Doherty, looking at Jake who was lying on the heather-strewn moss.
- 'Daydreaming,' said Jake.

They chortled in unison.

- 'Roger, what are dreams made of?' asked Jake, religiously laying his tiny pebble on the pile.
- 'Dreams are everywhere, around us, within us. They live through us and we live through them. We are part of them. We are a community made of dreams.
- Wow, that's lovely,' commented Beatrice.
- 'It's not me saying it, it's Master Khul,' said Doherty.
- 'Oh, yes. I've been hearing that name lately,' she said approvingly. 'And how do you know Taylor?
- Huh, what do you mean? Oh … Taylor! Yes, an old student of mine, why?' Doherty looked falsely confused.
- 'Will you be coming to the hotel with us, Mr. Doherty?' asked Jake sharply.
- 'I am in two minds about it. Then again, I think your uncle could do well with spending a night with the monk to expand his spirituality. Besides, someone needs to watch Dubois. I can't let them down.'

All three returned to the camp to build the sepulchre and the hearth around the fire. Jake and Beatrice looked at each other with anguish. At the camp,

Jonathan had made a start at the hearth and a stone hut, but the wind had picked up and the rampart around Dubois's body looked flimsy.

- 'There's a hot spring nearby,' said the monk Hashita, 'I will go and have a bath.'

Beatrice walked over to Jonathan and scooted on a large rock next to him. She saw his body bent over a few rocks that he was picking up painstakingly.

- 'Unk, I forgot to mention seeing Doherty speaking to Taylor at the aquarium, in Yokohama. It completely went out of my mind!
- Doherty spoke to whom?
- Taylor, the guy we met at the graveyard … Oh, I see, the famous graveyard fling, hey?' he said, jokingly.
- 'Taylor and Doherty met. Are you digging what I am saying?' she said.

Beatrice related how Doherty and Taylor had been conniving, how she had been listening in on their conversation.

- 'The fucking …It might be nothing, Unk. Doherty says he's a student of his, but I heard what I heard. He said "she's the chosen one."
- "She's the chosen one," talking about you, hey? I'll question him about it. I promise you, Bee. Then, we'll see who's the chosen one!' said Jonathan.

Towards noon, Beatrice and Jake buckled their rucksack excitedly and said goodbye to the rest of the camp. The three men posed in statelyness, imbued with a sense of magnanimous sacrifice as Jake and Beatrice walked down the trail towards civilisation. It took them the whole afternoon to reach the hotel La Vista, the first lodge they encountered on their way down.

The sight of the hammerbeam Norman style roof in the reception hall and its rustic interior felt familiar. Beatrice and Jake checked in and loitered in the hall for a few minutes, admiring the architecture, questioning silently the qurikiness of the European interior theme. But because of a certain pandemic, the hotel would be shutting its doors soon, according to a sign placarded on the unmanned reception desk. Jake and Beatrice looked in wonderment at the dark beams and stained crossmembers supporting the unusually high ceiling of the empty hotel.

- 'I do recommend the ice theme restaurant, it's a great dive,' said a voice behind Beatrice.

She turned around to face the man standing behind her, surprised by the proximity of his breath, close to her ear. She thought she recognised his voice:

- 'Taylor!' she exclaimed.
- 'Yep! I'm surprised you even remember my name. How have you been?' said Taylor, a beaming smile printed on his rubicund face, stretching his traits to hilarious proportions.

Jake gave him a suspicious look, which Beatrice noted, but strangely, she was too happy to see a familiar face and dismissed Jake's reaction as overprotective. Taylor showered her with excitement about the ice-themed restaurant. Beams and uprights, tables and chairs, walls made of ice. But it was Taylor, the cult member she soon realised, although Beatrice was blown away by the magical crystal palace illusion, a restaurant with ice tables and chairs …

- 'Shall I book a table for tonight?' said Taylor, euphoric.

Beatrice turned down his offer, using Jake as an excuse, but felt guilty.

- 'Are you sure? It could be fun, besides, I have some campers treats for you, in my room. Do you remember that night in Sydney? You left me in the lurch in the morning. It's all under the bridge now, but you owe me a solid!' he said, insistent.
- 'Oh, that night? I was jetlagged, it was all a bit too much. Plus, Jake doesn't like being challenged by unknown faces, you know.
- Oh, I'm sorry … But is he your little brother or something? He can come tonight too, if he wants!' said Taylor.
- 'No, thanks, Taylor. We're actually here on a mission to liaise with the hospital, a man has died on the team.

- You're kidding! All the more reasons to change scenery. Don't be such a tight ass … I am sorry, Taylor, I can't.'

Beatrice was hesitating, but felt she had a responsibility towards Jake and her uncle not to stray from her mission. Taylor honed in on her indecisiveness.

- 'Don't ditch again, Bee. Seriously?' Taylor was pressing her with bravado and charm, bearing on her body with his large shoulders.
- 'Jake, please go and drop the luggage off, will you? I won't be long, just the time for a drink and a chat. I promise you, I will take you to dinner.
- I'm not sure,' said Jake, troubled.
- 'Come on Jake, can't you take care of yourself for an hour, while I treat that young chick to a well-deserved break?' said Taylor, hypocritically suave.
- 'I won't be long, I promise,' said Beatrice.

Jake carried their luggage to the lift and looked back at them. His mind was overridden with doubt and anguish. He darted remonstrating glances at the tall, tawny board-shouldered soccer hunk and walked into the lift willy-nilly but didn't let Beatrice out of his sight until the door closed.

As the night went by, Beatrice's bedroom door opened abd closed twice. Jake heard the shower, Beatrice coming back from her night out with Taylor, several hours later, in the middle of the night. He did venture out of the bedroom to order a burger but Beatrice wasn't in the hotel. He searched all evening, called her several times too, but she didn't answer her phone. He finally fell asleep while revisiting his photos from Australia. In the morning, he was awaken by a knock on the door. It was Beatrice.

- 'Sorry, Jake. I didn't see your messages. Taylor and I had a little party.
- Are you serious? What about the aquarium, have you forgotten?
- I am entitled to let some steam off, you know. All in good time, Jake. I'll let you in on the gossip over breakfast. Come on, it's nearly nine!' said Beatrice.

Beatrice was distant albeit unapologetic all the way down to the breakfast room. Jake had a burning question on his mind and dark circles under his eyes too, but refrained from asking embarassing questions.

- 'Before you ask, Jaky, nothing happened between me and Taylor. Actually, I had an argument with him last night, about him and Doherty meeting at the aquarium. He was adamant it didn't happen. It all started well. He was charming and funny and then became insistent. Then, he was drunk out of his wits. Gosh, I was so stupid! Fortunately, the staff at his hotel was very helpful. One of them drove me back and Taylor was warned they wouldn't hesitate to call the police if he was harassing me again!
- Why didn't you wake me up?
- Precisely because I didn't want to wake you up Jake. It doesn't mean you're not my hero,' she said reassuringly.

She laid her hand on his arm to comfort him.

- 'I called the hospital and the storm is too violent up there. A rescue team found them by chance, but wasn't equipped to take away the body. They are coming down to organise a Heli rescue. They're saying that Unk, the monk and Doherty have been building a stone hearth hut and made a fire, but that they're running low on food. They did think about leaving Dubois behind but their sense of duty has prevailed so far!' said Beatrice, with an empathic flourish on the last words. 'I must say, this expedition is beginning to look like a horror movie,' said Beatrice, suddenly grave.
- 'Well, I didn't have fun last night either, you know, I looked for you everywhere. Let's just not talk about it. I'm eating now. Let's forget it. Let's make sure the hospital take that body away, that we find the flower so I can go home!' said Jake.

In Beatrice's room, beef stew cans laid on top of her bed table. Taylor had left them in front of her door, as some kind of sordid apology. She had looked at the cans and had felt preyed upon. Inside one of the cans, a bot fly larvae was boring holes in the juices looking for some meat to latch on to …

Wake's End

The flesh of their presence, the vertigo of the next world hanging over the precipice … It wasn't long before there was a storm. Their last powdered vegetable soups were boiling away in the pot, inside the stone hut they had built. Three nights had passed since Dubois's death and the winds had made it impossible for Toboku central hospital to charter a doctor-helicopter. An expedition had been sent to retrieve the body, but the storm had delayed them. Jonathan, keen herbalist since his retirement, had suggested foraging to find preservative wild plants while the flying doctor and rescue team tried to reach them to take Dubois' corpse away. It had been suggested that the body should be covered with branches and thick sleeping bags to avoid the birds of prey making a feast of Dubois's remains. Everyone agreed a retreat was imminent if the storm got worse. The question of Dubois' wake hanged like a sword of Damocles over their heads. Even tents were barely hanging by a thread and stones would be needed to ensure their safety against the elements. Under the whooshing gales, the tents began to clatter and clack. Trenches had been dug, but the camp was nevertheless exposed to the brewing storm, on a plateau, on the East side, where the eastern winds began howling, whistling and trilling forcefully.

- 'Our private *al fresco* chamber of death,' said Jonathan, sheltering from a gust of wind, his face dripping with the growing mizzle.
- 'It's so cold, I can barely feel my feet,' grunted Doherty.

Doherty was peering into the fire …

- 'A penny for the kingdom of your thoughts, Doherty,' Jonathan exhaled warm breath, looking at it fighting its chances with the cold air.
- 'You're gonna need more than the whole gold in the world to know my thoughts, I'm afraid,' whimpered Doherty, 'It's too cold to think.'

- 'What about you, Monk?' said Jonathan.

Hashita kept his thoughts to himself as the wake of the body of Dubois had started in earnest for him. Doherty signed.

- 'Are you a Catholic, Doherty?' asked Jonathan.
- 'I was raised one, yes.'

They chewed on tough meat …

- 'Gosh, I'm so bloody hungry I could eat the moon,' grunted Jonathan.
- 'I heard that food is tasteless in space. I wonder what Bezos would taste like,' said Doherty, chewing with his mouth open, haggard from the biting cold.
- 'Those jerkies sure taste like your humour,' sneered Jonathan.
- 'It's important not to lose sight of the hearth,' commented Hashita, reprovingly.
- 'I wonder if we shouldn't cremate the poor bugger, as an auto-da-fé,' suggested Doherty.
- 'He's neither a heretic, nor a Hindu, is he?' said Hashita, befuddled.
- 'Can we all let ourselves be stirred by this grave moment and stop the canting, before someone passes the bucket around?' said Jonathan, humorously.

The last of the wafer-thin crackers and the dried meat vanished before their eyes …

- 'This is the last night for me. I'm out of here tomorrow. They'll never come in that weather,' whined Doherty, shivering.
- 'Nah, we have to come to them,' agreed Jonathan.
- 'I will stay,' announced Hashita solemnly, pulling on the straps of his hood.
- 'Well, thanks for your brave decision, Mr. Hashita. We are grateful for your sacrifice indeed, but we don't want another body on our conscience,' said Doherty.

- 'Aye, it shouldn't take more than a day of two to complete formalities. Are you sure you don't want to come with us to the hotel?' asked Jonathan, standing up on his feet to warm himself up, trying to appeal to the monk's common sense.
- 'You sleep. I wake,' said Hashita resolute.
- 'Would you say a few words for the wake then, Master Hashita?' pleaded Jonathan.

The monk fidgeted and rolled on his buttocks before clearing his throat:

- 'His spirit is half-way there … It's been three days, and in seven days, it will reach paradise. The spirit will join its ancestors, who will take him. His soul is now leaping forward to the next world. We must help him make the steps … The Lord is taking him, whispering his soothing commands,' prayed Doherty.
'The spirits will welcome him, the mirror of his life on earth will face him … The Lord opens his arms, I can feel it,' added Doherty.

They all prayed together in silence.

- 'I wonder if Dubois wanted this to happen so much that he dreamt it,' argued Jonathan, after a long meditating pause.
- 'Famous last words: my corpse on a mountain? I don't think so,' argued Doherty. 'Who would want such an end, away from civilisation? Pecked by birds of prey and far from your loved ones?' said Doherty.
- 'He seemed very preoccupied. I should have checked his heart. To say that I had some digoxin, made from Foxglove!' said Jonathan, regretful, stirring the fire, 'I made it myself.
- Weren't the Japanese and the nazis hand in hand during WWII?' asked Doherty, quizzical.
- 'How is that relevant?' eructed Jonathan.
- 'Just thinking that I am paying the price for my gall in taking up my place on this expedition,' argued Doherty.
- 'And?' interrogated Jonathan, 'What does that have to do with Dubois lying down below?'

Jonathan glanced at Hashita for a reaction. The monk's eyes were closed.

- 'I am wondering whether Dubois wanted to make a point … And I am feeling sick for the victims of the nuclear bomb, that's all,' Doherty defended himself, 'Maybe, it's his thousand cranes statement.
- You're out of your mind, Doherty. And I'm not sure it's entirely due to the freezing cold!
- And why not? After all, the Japanese might have felt threatened enough by the Western world's enslavement of natives around the world to feel they had to push them back? Was the bomb warranted? Have we learnt our lessons?
- Does that make Dubois a martyr? I don't know, but I'd like to make sure I am able to tell the tale,' Jonathan philosophized. 'So Hashita san, will you come down the mountain with us or not?'
- 'Let's go to bed,' said Hashita, 'Tomorrow, I make a decision.'

The night shroud over the waking men was soon transmuted into softly palpable clouds by the morning lights. None of them slept because of the cold. All except Jonathan had gone to bed, trying to sleep in earnest. Pointless in that cold though, had decreted Jonathan. In the morning, one of those clouds, a long and soft mass of dark tufty wool, looked like an asparagus hanging over the top of the hills below, thought Jonathan. Then again, it could have been a spear or a bird's foot. As he waited for Doherty and Hashita to raise from their couch, he felt the weight of Dubois's death leaving his shoulders, taking flight like a spirit in the thawing sky. Soon, he would leave but a dearth of evidence for his existence behind. He felt for a sign in his pockets and found Dubois's last Dunhill cigarettes. Soon, the asparagus turned into a mouse, then a sheep's head with an elongated body that made him smile, and as the two men came to his side, the cloud turned into little fish before becoming again a formless cloud.

Stones were dripping with sweet mineral goodness in the morning sleet. Jonathan felt the substance of life on earth, molecules of rare gases made fluid by the grace of the universe. He felt it melting on his shoulders.

- 'We need to take care of our own body, you know,' said Doherty, tightening his belt. 'I've already lost a pound.'

Jonathan and Hashita huddled by the fire that Jonathan had kept alive all night. He had been covering Dubois with another spare tent canvass, tucking the body of the old French anthropologist under with rocks. Fortunately, the winds had been clement to Dubois, as they flattened against the rock face before reaching his body. He went down to check on him. As he touched Dubois' hand, he realised one of his fingers were missing. It seemed it had been chewed off ...

- 'There's little wood left. There's only moss and it's wet. I can go back down to fetch some more but we might as well go back to the tree line and the hotel,' said Doherty, eager to convince the monk it was time to go.

Hashita looked at the precipice:

- 'It's the same substance that animates our body with electricity ... We are mere conductors of the wider spirit of the world,' mused the monk, looking at the frail silhouette of Deadstone, standing by Dubois in the morning slush.
- 'It's all pretty fucked as far as Dubois's concerned,' said Jonathan, as he looked up at the sky, now warming up his hands by the dying fire. 'He's already missing a finger.'

Master Hashita now stood in between the two men sitting, dripping and strangely stoic despite the cold.

- 'Master Hashita, you have to come with us! We can't leave you here. You know, it's unreasonable. Dubois has left this world,' said Jonathan, looking up, raising his head towards Hashita.
- 'No, Mr. Deadstone, it's what you knew as Mr. Dubois that has left this world, and you cannot accept he has not travelled to the next world yet,' said Hashita.

Doherty jumped on the bandwagon of spirituality to posit himself as a mediator.

- 'A body needs burying though, otherwise before long, it will harbour diseases …The snowflake western spirit makes you lose sight of the bigger picture, here gentlemen,' said the monk in a surprisingly fluid English.
- 'What do you make of your own body, Hashita san? Before long, you'll catch death if you stay here! And what about us then? How will we find the flower?' said Doherty.
- 'I say nothing … When your God speaks, he speaks to your hearts. I would let the heart speak, if that's what your God mean, why don't you let it?
- My heart is torn between Dubois's wishes and the concrete necessity. We're out of food. There won't be emergency services coming our way, because of that damned Covid virus! We are stuck here with a half-frozen body! We can't bury the poor fellow against his wishes,' argued Jonathan, irritated at Doherty and Hashita's existentialist jives.
- 'What is Christian trinity?' asked the monk, dubious about Doherty's motives.
- 'I suppose it's a narcissistic triangle,' submitted Jonathan facetiously.
- 'I believe Jesus is the God women can identify to,' said the monk, satisfied with his remark.
- 'And?' Doherty pressed Hashita.
- 'He means empathy, surely,' said Jonathan.
- 'What if Dubois had anticipated this and wanted to be part of the Gaia reality, the God-mother earth where everything is recycled into something else?' suggested Doherty. 'It would certainly explain all this. He might have meant to be eaten away!'
- 'Rightly said, Doherty. His wishes were clear. Mr. Dubois wanted nothing more than for his body to rot and whittle away in the wind and snow,' Jonathan concurred to Doherty's surprise.
- 'But, what about his spirit?' said Hashita.
- 'His spirit is the angel's share, whatever is left after everything is said and done,' argued Jonathan, now sombre again.
- 'Waky, waky, western world, here's the new psychological revolution,' scoffed Doherty.
- 'But his spirit is alive still, isn't it?' suggested Hashita, concerned.
- 'It lives on through our memory and nothing else,' pondered Jonathan.

Hashita and Doherty looked at each other, disconfited.

- 'Then, we can't go,' argued Hashita triumphantly.
- 'No, on the contrary, let's leave camp,' said Jonathan. 'Let's leave this mortal coil behind and be content with his body being eaten. His spirit will find its way. I suppose that's what Dubois's testament was, even if it doesn't sit well with our Christian upbringing or your Buddhist respect for the passing of the dead. His spirit will live on as a figment of our imagination.
- Maybe, he felt he had the virus and wanted to protect us all,' said Doherty, clutching at the last straw.
- 'To say he couldn't help thinking like myself that this virus was man-made run-away lab experiment. Damn biological war!' said Jonathan.
- 'What on earth do you mean, Dr. Deadstone?' interjected the monk, whose curiosity had been piqued. 'Do you not accept diseases such as the flu, you, a medical man?'

The monk's head was bobbing in disbelief…

- 'Of course, I do. But I mean, we are in the midst of a biological war, stuck between the East and the West's battle for philosophical supremacy after all. I could be wrong. I guess I am just tired of this camp, I suppose.
- So, it's final then, we move and leave Dubois's body behind. I didn't come here to play funeral undertakers,' said Doherty.
- 'What do you think, Mr. Hashita?' asked Jonathan.
- 'You're right! Something's off with this pandemic. There was a virus out there, in 2003, the same virus was around and it didn't become a world issue. Yet, people already travelled by plane in 2003. It doesn't make sense. And again, in 2012, in the Middle-East. And all of a sudden, a vaccine appears out of the fridge. Strange coincidence. I genuinely think that humanity is trying to find new ways of destroying itself. This is where I draw the line. This is where my mission begins and ends,' said Hashita.

The monk tilted his head towards Jonathan, as if he did not expected an answer. He looked at the vast expanse of sky above their head:

- 'There's a purpose to it all, I guess. We have been made to believe that it was a fatality, but the world is nevertheless anxious about overpopulation. We're being made redundant by nature. I say, respect Dubois's wishes, go back to civilisation and get a rest. I know a place that will take us, still open for business. Then, Hashita can take us to the flower. We need to show the world that there's an outer path, a way out of the destruction,' urged Doherty.

He wiped the palms of his hand on his knees, satisfied with his conclusions.

- 'So that's that then, let's see what the flower has to say about all that. I am partial to a good bath when the shit hits the fan. I'd be grateful for it. At least, the Trinity college won't bother us. Jim Walden can go fuck himself,' said Jonathan.
- 'Righto, I hate to say it, but this pandemic is a blessing in disguise. Let's honour Dubois's wishes and show the holier-than-thous that they do not have all the answers for us. I'm glad we came to our senses in the end. I can already feel my mind expanding to new circles of consciousness just sitting here, in the rain … I can't wait to see that flower,' said Doherty.
- 'But, what if it's the flower that caused Dubois's death? What do you think about that?' asked the monk moralizingly.

Jonathan and Doherty sat stil, looking at each other in disbelief.

- 'The flower only reveals what's in your heart, you said it yourself,' said Doherty.
- 'Master Khul said it too,' said Jonathan.
- 'Or Dubois said it, hard to say really,' said Hashita. 'This is why we need to cleanse ourselves, so there is no surprise. At least, we can all agree on that. We have to retreat, accept we are not ready.'

Doherty stood up slowly, waiting for the other two men to do the same:

- 'So let's go chaps! I need that food! Let's figure out what is happening in this world, after a good bath and a good meal, we'll see even clearer!
- Try the hot springs, sirs, before you go, then we can leave at noon, in the full light of our refreshed spirits,' said Hashita.

The three men bathed in the hot springs some few hundred yards from Dubois's body. Keeping dry as much as they could in the rain, they walked from noon to the evening. Towards the afternoon, the sun made a reappearance. They were half-way towards the foot of the mountain when Hashita broke their silence:

- 'Ō-Asahidake, the Japanese name of the mountain is one of the hundred most famous, and probably the most famous in Japan, after Mount Fuji. It's the highest peak in Hokkaido,' explained Hashita.

The men took in their mind and soul the vibrancy of the Garden of the Gods around them, a flora and fauna so intensely enchanting that they felt surrounded by a carpet of spring tidings, just waiting for their spirit to walk into its kaleidoscopic fantasia. Jonathan spotted a skunk cabbage, a flower that resembles a lily:

- 'Hashita san, this flower is a lily, isn't it?
- Oh, yes, it's called Mitzubasho, it announces spring.'

Jonathan noticed the foul smell of the flower. It was called skunk cabbage for a reason. The Marsh marigolds and the alpine avens were also sprouting.

- 'We need to get Beatrice and prepare our ascent,' said Doherty.

Jonathan perceived in his voice an unwholesome interest for the girl.
- 'What is it that you want from Beatrice, Doherty? The kids heard you talk to Taylor about Beatrice, what was that about?' asked Jonathan agitatedly.
- 'I mean everyone, let's join everyone down there, Hashita san,' said Doherty, evading Jonathan's probing.

- 'I understand that I need to cleanse myself. May I bother you for a meditation, among this beautiful scenery? Hashita san?' said Doherty.
- 'I would eagerly join you,' said Jonathan, still suspicious of Doherty.
- 'Dr. Deadstone, may I ask you about Beatrice? I understand she's your family, isn't she?' said Hashita.
- 'Yes, my niece, well, no, my cousin actually. She's the daughter of my Aunt who's financing this expedition. Dubois must have mentioned her.
- Oh, so, so, so … He did mention. She's very pretty, isn't she?
- A stunner, if you ask me,' said Doherty.
- 'Yes, she is. I am very fond of her …I noticed that you have eyes on her.
- I have eyes on her, yes! If that's what you mean …Oh, so, so, so … ' The monk smiled as his eyes disappeared behind his eyebrows.
- 'Would you care sharing, Hashita san?' asked Jonathan.
- 'It's Jake I am not sure about, you see … No offense.
- None taken!' blurted Jonathan.
- 'I see … ' said Hashita, with sagaciousness.
- 'What about here?' suggested Doherty, showing a bush, blessed by a sunny halo of light.

They sat by a bush of yellow rhododendrons, bearing the promise of summer buds.

- 'I think this is perfect! The rhododendron's leaves are tinctured and used to treat many conditions. It's perfect for my rheumatism,' boasted Jonathan.

Doherty sat down in his lotus position with the monk. Jonathan struggled to imitate them at first, and settled for the Indian position. The city of Shitakara's smokes below could be seen writhing towards the sky.

Soon, they reached the La Vista hotel. A few guests were taking their luggage out, as the hotel was closing down. Most of them had already made plans to stay at a lodge further down the hill, where individual pods enabled social distancing.

Laughter and Squealing

Jonathan sleepwalked to the toilets, arms slightly raised to avoid imminent obstacles such as ajar doors, chairs left in the passage ways, and bean bags planted by wee badgers. Ever since he was a sleepwalker, his little brother James had mischieviously laid obstacles on his way to see if he would avoid them if his eyes were closed.

For the first time, since he was ten, he walked towards the bathroom, making sure to pick up the bottle of milk his father had left on the kitchen worktop in case he was thirsty during the night. Reaching out for what he thought was the bottle of milk, he took the can of beef stew gifted to him by Beatrice the night before, opened the can and emptied the content in his stomach. He was woken up by a bulky recalcitrant morsel of beef.

In his dreams, he had sleepwalked to the bathroom, and let his memory wander to his childhood days and the safety of his parents' home. It wasn't by chance that he fell in and out of sleep that night. He was now responsible for the young people he had taken to this foreign land. His first priority was the safety of Beatrice and the fact that anything could happen once they were faced with the Everblue. He felt a pang of regret, thinking that Catherine Hallmark, his aunt, would never forgive him if he put her daughter's life at risk.

When he realised he was holding the can of stew that lay on his bedside table instead of the bottle of milk, he rolled down the side of the bed and crashed on the floor, his right leg first, leaning on the table so as to arrest his fall but slipped, spilling the rest of the can amidst the crashing sound of his body on the floor of his hotel bedroom.

His painful landing on the wooden floor woke him up. He couldn't repress a feeling of anger towards his little brother. As he climbed back into bed, he sighed. His little brother was innocent this time. A strange feeling overwhelmed him, like a hurt that he had been hiding, or a painful memory that needed casting away. He felt for his leg, half-awake, intent on going back to sleep. There would be a bruise in the morning there too.

His whiskey days in the solitude of his private chambers in Eden Borough were not news, but the emperor's clothes had now a strange smell of sweat and death. He had been revisiting his childhood in his sleep, dispelling Dubois' death as yet another hypnopompic hallucination. Now, he munched on the last morsel of meat trying to resume his slumbering journey.

The fact that, according to his parents, no incident ever happened while he sleepwalked had always amazed him. His parents had moved house just after his ninth birthday. The family had settled peacefully in their new home, around the Lochrin basin, in the little Eden Borough street. The new property was similar in shape to any other houses in Scotland, as was often the case among the working class. But his life would never be the same after that night when his little brother followed him round the streets of Eden Borough's basin in his pyjamas. He reckoned the scaring thought of deambulating half-naked in the streets near the canal had cured him of his somnambulist habit for good.

The new house was a two up two down terrace. No surprise there. His mother, who always slept soundly, had given up overseeing her child's sleepwalking, but as the happy-go-lucky bohemian spirit she was, on top of her long shifts at the hospital, she was determined to sleep throughout that night without disturbance. She was confident nothing would ever happen to him since both his parents had observed his nightly routine many times before. They had surprised him several times in the middle of the night, and knew that his nocturnal escapades were always short trips around the house, mainly from the bedroom to the kitchen or the bathroom.

The first time Jonathan was seen sleepwalking, his mother and father were shocked, of course. They had never heard of somnanbulism in their family. Seeing the wee lad walking in his sleep around the house after he just turned five gave his "maw" quite a fright. If Jonathan was the first in the family to ever do the noctambulist walk, after numerous sightings, his parents decided that he had become a seasoned night traveller and actually noticed nothing again for years until that night …In fact, his little brother had played tricks on Jonathan for years before that fateful night by the canal. The last time he had done just that had created quite a stir in the household and Mr. Deadstone, his father, had duly admonished the wee boy for his tasteless joke, once he not-so-involuntary vented out the details in front of the family's kitchen tribunal.

After Jonathan's ninth birthday, a strange thing happened, however …For this new home, his mother had innocently decided the lounge and reception rooms layouts had to be changed. Her *avantgarde* women magazines, with their fancy fashion and good housekeeping tips, had given her grand ideas about remodelling her home interior. Her head full of novel designs, she stubbornly set on making her house more modern, away from the traditional sofa-TV hot and cold corners layout. The reception cum dining room middle-of the-room-center-piece-table malarkey also had to be turned around. She had simply forgotten about her wee lad's nocturnal habits.

Jonathan raised from his slumber in the new house—arms of a sleepwalker are not raised as commonly believed, in front of them, but stretched out only through door frames—and had begun sleepwalking, taking to the new home like a fish to water as expected, happy to ramble around at night as he had always done, sometimes having a "blether" to himself in the process. But that night, nine-year-old Jonathan opened the front door and walked towards the canal … The commotion due to the new layout had raised the alarm with his little brother who followed him dutifully, making sure not to wake him up as he had been severely reminded to do. Feeling guilty from his own treatment of his big brother, he followed him around conscientiously. That night, he saw Jonathan walking along the basin, and, jolting behind him, painfully constricted and conflicted, tried not to wake him, pestering against his predicament, keeping an eye on his big brother's every step:

- 'Aargh, dinnae go down there, Johno! For Christ's sake!'

Remembering his dad's stark warning and threatening paw in front of his face:

- 'Aargh, Haud your weescht, you stupid … ' (He remembered his mother telling him off too)

Jonathan walked for two miles around the basin, swerving around and over obstacles while his brother cantered behind him, sometimes pussy-footing ahead in agony about doing anything at all to prevent a catastrophe, frightfully weary of the proximity of water. At last, it looked like his big brother would return to their home on Grove street, unharmed. Except for a couple of late-night revellers who cheered them up on their way, and who threatened to do them in a few blocks later, Jonathan came home safe and sound. Jonathan smiled in his sleep, remembering the joyous storytelling of his night escapade around the kitchen table, the cheers and the laughs of his sibling and parents, as the story was told again and again …

The lodge was quiet, apart from the clanking sound of the central heating pipes knocking against the wooden boards, which made the woodwork vibrate. The stew had been tasty. *American stew*, he dreamt, *can't beat American stew*. Jonathan had not slept in a bed since the camp on Asahi mount. He finally dozed off in a comfortable dwam. The lodge's wooden frames were cracking under the wind. The monk was right. A cleansing was necessary before the ascension. He would have to talk to Beatrice and Jake, insisting on their own cleansing too. What did that entail exactly? And how was he supposed to talk to Jake into cleansing? The autistic wee lad promised to be a challenge. He would say "amen" to everything but would understand little of what the Everblue really meant at all. He remembered what the monk had said about him: '*It's Jake I am not sure about.*'

What did he mean by that?

Jonathan suddenly got up and washed his face in front of the mirror, unable to shake off his concerns. The feeling of the cold water on his cheeks and hands dispelled any residual doubts about being a kid again. He dried his hands with the fresh towel, thinking about his little brother who, like him, had had his own nocturnal habits. Jonathan would speak to him in his sleep. Whole conversations with him while his little brother was asleep, he had. He would make sure to find out all his secrets. Dream-spying. It must have been the beginning of his psychoanalysis streak, he assumed. Already, as a child, he was interested in the paranormal, the subconscious world seen from the standpoint of reality, the mind and memory. It was all so fascinating. Of course, his brother never remembered anything, just like he never remembered anything about his own sleepwalking trips.

The surface of the hot spring bath of the Las Vista lodge was still and lukewarm, smoke rising like a spirit. The distant clatter of chit chat of women bathing their feet in the tranquility of their intimate bonding and the guests' introspective murmurs during the day had all but fell silent, absorbed by Mother Nature like a buffer, making way for the silent world of dreams.

He walked back to his bed and laid down, still exhausted after the three nights spent on top of Asahi mount. He went back to bed straightway, clinching his pillow like a baby hangs on to the sleeves of his breastfeeding mother. But Jonathan found it hard to go back to sleep fully, as he heard a laughter that he began to identify as a subdued anodyne masculine chortle at first, but that gradually intensified into a deranged disembodied snicker, reverberating in the corridors and hollow spaces of the lodge.

The sound wasn't coming from his memory or the remembrance of the previous day's auditory landscape. He didn't recognize the voice as something familiar, nor was it unfamiliar. It had this strange homely tone about it that he couldn't quite place. He had never heard it before, whether in the lodge or anywhere else during his lifetime, yet couldn't dismiss it as completely foreign. It didn't belong to his dreams either as his eyes were now opened to the dark pine panelling of the ceiling.

The canned laughter soon turned into a snickering chortle, then amplified to a cruel, pernicious giggle, filling the room and all spaces around him, as if it knew where to land when he wasn't listening. The terrible jittering chortle soon invested the void of his mind. He felt as if the voice had been carved from his own self, emerging from his soul and splashed like a sordid soundscape on his sensory world. The terryfying revelation of this deranged laughter was that he couldn't be sure it came from within or without. You simply cannot imagine a voice like that coming from anywhere else than outside, yet, it resonated inside, as if a sadistic audio-engineer had contrived to make it resonate inside his head. He must have been involved in that process at some point but couldn't remember when. *But only in cases of schizophrenia, right*? He told himself repeatedly. Last time he checked, he was the one dishing out sanitary advice about other people's heads.

He was sure everyone was still asleep, but began doubting he was actually awake … He had to acknowledge that loud laughter now. How else? He was perfectly sane a few hours ago, and these conditions don't just pop up out of nowhere. By now, his breath was so shallow that he had to take a deep breath to submerge back again into oxygenated reality. Jonathan knew that the laughter had nothing to do with his own voice, that it was alien to his own psychological makeup, alien to his vocal identity. It was a man's laughter, for sure, but not his.

Meanwhile the laughter gained in intensity. It became even louder, insane, uncontrollable; its origins still being denied to him. But outside, no commotion, no stir, just a silent hotel in the middle of nowhere, or so it seemed. And so he checked. He got up, peered through the window of his bedroom into the dark corridor. He could see no one. He couldn't feel any presence, despite his senses being heightened. The laughter definitely didn't come from outside his bedroom. He checked again by successively closing and opening the door of his room, but saw no one. He listened to doors down the corridor, but couldn't see anyone or feel anything moving. Besides, the laughter had stopped as soon as he had opened the door. It should have been extraneous to his senses, which it wasn't. His own mouth was closed. He cupped his hands to his ears but the laughter was as loud as ever. He felt on the cusp of insanity despite mustering his resolve …It went on without abating until he went to the bathroom fumbling for earplugs that he knew he had placed in his Pierre Cardin's leather vanity case. He put them on hurriedly, checking he wasn't sleepwalking by quickly glancing into the mirror by passing and washing his face again with fresh cold water from the tap. The laughter had stopped. It must have disappeared, somehow. But whether it reverberated as soon as he turned off the lights, or whether it was already in his head, lurking for a moment of distraction, he could not tell, but as sure as his body was tensely waiting for the laughter to start again, his senses prone like a special forces on a mission in enemy territory, he heard it again. He felt himself panting, associating his pulse with the foreign sound that no one but him could hear. His psychiatric mind waited patiently for a reasonable explanation until he had to admit that he could not find any, while the laughter went on as loud as the flow of water in a shower room, then as loud as the engine of a car, then as loud as a storm, then as loud as a volcano roaring through the thickness of his skin:

- 'Stop it!' he yelled.

The sound coming out of his mouth was so harsh and intense that he felt the shock of his energy leaving his body, prone on his elbows, on his bed, in the midnight prayer's position. He lied down again, coiled, as he heard himself whine like a sick dog. The laughter stopped again when he felt his blood rushing to his temples, his pulse knocking against his arteries as if they were about to burst. Suddenly, a loud shriek forced him to stand on his two feet with his fists clenched, looking around for the intruder. He waited for a few seconds that felt like minutes, freaked out, waiting for the terrible laughter to assault his senses again …Until the lodge got busy with people waking up, until the clatter of pipes and noises of water flowing from the showers around the hotel could be heard, he waited wilfully for the memory of that laughter to vanish with the light of day. The laughter wasn't heard again.

When he got up again, Jonathan's foot foundered on a metallic milk bottle cap left on the floor of his room. He looked at it with astonishment. He had not brought a bottle of milk into his room. He didn't drink milk. After he finished showering and dressing up, he tried to work out where the bottle of milk fitting the cap could be until he heard a knock on the door and opened his bedroom to Beatrice. He had asked her to wake him up the night before. The sight of her broke the spell. It felt like a relief after his hallucinatory dream:

- 'Bee, did you hear a loud laughter last night, towards the early hours of the morning?' he asked, feeling awkward.
- 'A laughter? No. I slept like a baby. Freaked out, you? I would never have thought.
- Yeah … ' said Jonathan with a derisive snort.
- 'I didn't hear anything. Ask Jake next door maybe, he doesn't sleep until the small hours, plays video games or music on his tablet throughout the night, he does!
- Okay, I will … He probably heard it too,' said Jonathan.

Jonathan knew better than to ask Jake about the laughter he heard so loudly during the night. Beatrice could be trusted, but Jake? He remembered the monk warning him against the lad. At the breakfast table, he tried to find clues in Jake's attitude that could dispel his doubts about the laughter being more than a psychotic breakdown. Looking at Jake listening to his bowl of rice krispies like an Indian a train track, he dismissed the idea. The whole laughter investigation threatened to be no more than a stupid cinematic memory that would have given water to the mill of his hallucination. He looked at the monk for answers and Jake for a culprit:

- 'Don't look,' said Jake, 'but Jackson's here.'

Jonathan turned around to look at the guy Jakes was pointing to, his neck turned towards a young western man.

- 'Who's Jackson? Anything I should know, Beatrice?' asked Jonathan, looking out for any suspicious innuendo he had missed between Jake and Beatrice.
- 'I did say "don't look", groaned Jake in between his teeth, shaking his head derisively.
- It's okay, unclench your fists,' said Beatrice, comforting Jake, trying to avoid turning round.
- 'Taylor, now Jackson? Seriously,' said Jake.

Jackson, the Business school student, was bent over his bowl of cereals, glancing intermittently at the table. Jonathan tried to catch his eyes, but he was intently following Beatrice's every move and did not seem to notice anyone else.

- 'Unk, it's okay. It's my fault really. It's a long story, suffice to say that he won't cause any trouble, he's been warned too.
- Is he bothering you, that one?' said Jonathan.
- 'Not anymore, he won't,' said Beatrice.
- 'Well, let me know if he does,' said Jonathan.

He whispered in Beatrice's ears:

- 'Did you tell him about the flower, by any chance? Should we expect a crowd of suitors at the top of Asahi mount now? We won't enjoy this beautiful place for long, you know that, right?'

Beatrice was insulted by his ominous tone.

- 'I said it was okay!
- Not with him around,' blurted Jake, who had listened in on their side conversation.

Watching the people gathered around the table, he suddenly noticed Doherty was missing. It's while munching a bacon slice, looking at the monk painstakingly picking up his ant-size rice grains from his wooden bowl with his chopsticks that Jonathan realised the laughter he had heard the night before was a powerful omen he should not dismiss.

- 'Jake, can I talk to you?'

Jonathan rose from the table and waited for Jake to take off his phone earplugs.

- 'Huh?
- Can you and I have a chat, please?
- Er ... Okay,' said Jake diffidently, standing up with alacrity.

Surprised, Jake cast a desperate look at Beatrice before following Jonathan to the front reception and then to the entrance door until they stood outside in the bright spring sunlight.

- 'Jake, You didn't happen to hear a strong laughter in the night, did you?
- No, I didn't, why?
- I know you like to stay awake at night, ditto Beatrice, so did you or did you not ... hear someone laugh, really loudly?
- I did stay awake, but I had my earphones on ... I still would have heard something, especially in the night, right?
- How do you sleep at night, by the way?
- I just close my eyes and sleep, I guess ... No, silly, I mean, do you sleep well?
- Oh, no ... Not really, I stay awake until everyone else is asleep.
- I was a sleepwalker once, when I was a child,' said Jonathan.
- 'Really?' said Jake, as if he had emerged from an embarrassing quid-pro-quo.
- 'Yes, and my brother once had to follow me around town in his pyjamas (Jake smiled). It would have been funny if I remembered anything about it. But they told me the story. I mean, my parents ...You seriously can't remember anything when you sleepwalk, can you?
- No, did you ever sleepwalk at all yourself?
- Well, I wouldn't know, would I,' said Jake, fidgety, his body tense and energetically disturbed by the intimacy of Jonathan's confession.
- 'Well, your parents would have told you. Never mind, thanks. That's all I wanted to know. You may go back to whatever you were doing now.
- I never knew my parents. Didn't Beatrice tell you?

- No, sorry, I didn't know,' said Jonathan, unnerved.
- 'Are you okay, Mr. Deadstone?
- Yes, of course! Call me Jonathan, Jake. It's not like you don't know me by now, is it?'

Jonathan made a last-ditch attempt at confounding Jake:

- 'Was it you last night?' said Jonathan, snappily.
- 'What do you mean?' said Jake, ominously.
- 'The laughter!
- What laughter?
- Oh, forget it.'

Jonathan watched Jake's slouching shoulders and sherpa hoody scuttling away into the wood-paneled entrance of the lodge.

The monk had said of Jake: 'I'm not sure about him.' As he opened Dubois's pack of Dunhill cigarettes to take the last fag out, he noticed a bulge under his skin. All cigarettes had gone. He looked twice and ran his finger over it. It was moving, as if a throbbing vein was swelling. He turned his head away, looked again with fresh eyes. The bulge had disappeared.Still now were the winds that had blown them out of their wits on the mountain where Dubois was still lying. Jonathan looked up to the summit. He pictured his body offered to the natural elements. A false sense of security had gradually spread among the guests at the lodge as they prepared for the next leg of the journey. The ascent was scheduled for the day after tomorrow. The monk had decreted it should be so, and the weather seemed to corroborate his predictions.

His Method of Madness

Jake Edward-Angst was counting the stones pushed out from the boundary of the lodge's Zen gardens. They felt like a haiku, a short poem of truth, a poetic moment of calm and reflection feeding one's thoughts with blankness, as the eyes become hypnotised by the serenity and apparent randomness of fluid Zen lines. Jake waited for the monk to say the first word but it didn't seem like he would speak. Instead, Hashita stared at the winding lines left by the inspired gardener and breathed deeply, repeatedly, trying to impart a sense of calmness and tranquility to the young man.

Meditation in the lulling spring evening was not on Jake's agenda. Ever since the beginning of his adventure, he had watched over Beatrice as if she was his big sister. He was on a mission, resolved to see it through. Why did the monk have to call him over? What did he want from him? The monk acknowledged his presence by his side, on the bench facing the setting sun, where boundaries between the known and the unknown got blurred. At least, that's how the monk wanted Jake to feel.

- 'What will you have for dinner, now, Mr. Hashita? I quite fancy those dumplings they make with pork meat. What do you call them?
- So, so, so. In a moment. First, cleansing,' said Hashita, meditating or acting, Jake couldn't tell.

The monk nodded ceremoniously, his head bobbing for what seemed an eternity to Jake whose leg began shaking. The monk put a hand on his knee.

- 'Huh?
- Stop it!
- Hey, fuck off! you sanctimonious Buddha freak! You levitating shit!'

Jake glanced furiously at the monk and walked off, but couldn't help turning around one more time to serve another injurious salve at him:

- 'Bloody freak! With your fucking hands on my knee, you perv!' Jake shouted.

The monk smiled and kept staring at the garden, satisfied his suspicions about Jake were founded.

- 'We're leaving tomorrow, Doherty. Where have you been?'

Roger Doherty had dragged his sandals to the bar, where Jonathan was waiting for an Irish coffee. He had tried to explain to the green-eyed waitress how to make the drink, but the young buxom impersonation of a Japanese anime figurine was fumbling for excuses. She bustled behind the bar, visible taken aback by Deadstone's request.

- 'I fell into an ambush last night,' said Doherty, eating humble pie.

Jonathan turned round on his seat to face him.

- 'Are you okay?
- Oh, I'm okay, it's my wallet that hurts ... Argh ... Mony a mickle makes a muckle, as they say back home. What on earth did you get up to last night in town, hey?' said Jonathan.

Understanding that Doherty had been on a raunchy night out, the thought of teasing the old dog to extract a little for some juicy gossip suddenly seemed like a good distraction:

- 'Nothing that you wanna know about, I'm just here for a night cap, I'm going to bed as soon as the sun's down,' said Doherty.
- 'Well, it won't be for a little while yet. Would you care for a pick-me up on the house? You look like something the cat dragged in,' said Jonathan.
- 'Sure. Be my guest,' said Doherty, sternly.

- 'Make it two', said Jonathan to the waitress who needed facial confirmation that he wanted another of those tricky Irish coffees.
- 'So, Hashita has spoken to Jake and he's a time bomb. Some abuse issues, he says,' said Jonathan.
- 'You don't say! Not too keen on shop talk right now, my head hurts and my heart drowned in that lovely Geisha's eyes I spent the best part of the night with! A splendid beauty of the purest kind. I'd like to go to sleep on this lovely note, thank you very much, not some care kid's trauma.
- We're leaving tomorrow at dawn. Hashita wants to get to mid-point at noon, so that we can get to the flower by dusk. You remember Dubois' prescription, don't you?
- Which is?' asked Doherty, distractedly.
- 'The flower is to be seen at night.
- Damn, of course ... I'd better go to bed then, if it's another night under the stars we're looking at.
- Take it with you.
- What?

Jonathan pushed his own Irish coffee towards Doherty.

- Oh, thanks. More tomorrow ... Right now, I just can't.
- No bother,' said Jonathan.

At dinner, Jake and the monk found themselves caught in a Mexican stand off. Jonathan was talking to Beatrice about the next day's schedule and what to pack: food and whatever wooly stuff she could gather. Jake stood up and apologized, he wasn't feeling well.

- 'Have a goon night,' joked Beatrice.
- 'What have you been up to, today?' asked Jonathan.
- 'Those girls were absolutely the nicest people I have ever met. I had a meal at their house. I had to take off my shoes. We ate by the fire. The room was so smoky! It was eerie. The meal was fish, chicken, all sorts of delicious foods, and those bean cakes, Oh my God! I even came back

with a bag full of word-shopping in survival Japanese! I'm sure I can borrow a few pairs of woolly socks from them tonight.
- Great! Fantastic to know that you had a great day. But Jake is a worry, Bee …
- How so?
- The monk doubts he will hold his fire when the going gets tough.
- You speak in riddles, though, Unk … Why don't you guys speak to him in plain English! He understands the most complex things if the language is simple! That doesn't mean he can't imitate complex language too, he's really good at imitating,' said Beatrice.
- 'That's what I gathered. But, his reaction with the monk was violent,' said Jonathan.
- 'Violent? Jake wouldn't hurt a fly, unless I was the one getting hurt!
- Will you be okay watching him from now on?
- That's what I've been doing so far, Unk, in case you didn't notice …
- I know, I know … You're a good girl.

It suddenly felt to him that he might have knocked his head on the bedside table too last night. The milk bottle cap still didn't make sense either. Then again, he had forgotten how the sight and close proximity of Beatrice could make him feel dysfunctional. His blood ran twice as he saw her clear blue eyes:

- 'What is it, Unk?
- Hmm?
- An angel passed,' she said. Her voice was gentle and pregnant with innuendos.
- 'Oh, I have this hitch since we're at the lodge. It's my left arm, I feel like scratching to the bone. I have a remedy I could use, I just didn't get round to it. Observing I suppose … I need to find a chemist or go for a walk in the countryside to find some herbs!
- Well, don't let us down, Unk. I'm scared … I don't think I would be able to take it if you were to fall ill or something similarly sinister.
- I'll be fine, don't you worry!'

He put his hands around her shoulders and felt like kissing her, but refrained, stopped by the erythema on his arm, which had begun forming a blister.

- 'Bee, can you have a look at this with your eyes, and tell me what you see?

Beatrice took a close look at his arm:

- It looks like a little crater, a red crater with …
- Oh, ok, I see.
- What is it?
- I think it's an insect bite of some sort.'

At sunset, Jonathan went outside to breathe some fresh air after his visited his room and fetched an anti-inflammatory cream. His knowledge of the Japanese flora was insufficient. He could find herbs to treat his skin but would need to identify them first. He looked at the entrance of the lodge. It looked like an open mouth, gulping down guests as many an indolent blob unaware of their fate. He saw the monk Hashita coming out. He didn't notice he was being observed. He watched the thin-paper monk and his bald head follow the trail behind the one storey building, which spread out onto a natural plateau, carved at the bottom of the hill. The little trails leading to the onsen baths, continuously heated by volcanic groundwater, were hiding places for the fatigued souls of travellers seeking to blend in with the scenery. At the top of the hill, a temple and a few more gardens were providing tranquility and space for the body to vibrate to those illustrious rock-bound spirits of the ages.
For the first time, Jonathan felt grateful for the jet lag. He felt his body slowly acclimatizing to the ambient serenity of the place as in a waking dream. Nothing here seemed real. He glanced at his arm, unable to tell if the bulge was a cyst or a vesicle …

Night, Night …

'Ronc, shhh, ronc, shhh, ronc, ronc, ronc.'

Roger Doherty was lying on his bed, flat on his pooch, his open mouth dribbling on a white pillow case … The sounds of the hotel and guests around him ricocheted in the wiring of his brains as he safely coiled up to find overdue sleep. No sounds were seeping through the deepest recoils of his mind, however. Instead, they danced and mixed somewhere in his frontal lobe, waiting for a ride home.

As the night fell and the hotel became silent again, save for a couple of late night owls dragging the moon over the edge of night, raising a cain as they waddled back to their bedroom, Doherty's brain began soaking up the distant sounds as if they were part of the flow of his dreams, taking them all in, making a neural soup of half-naked fantasies and memories that his wanderlust devoured with pleasure and curiosity.

His debauchery companion the previous night had green eyes … She had opened his chakras. Doherty remembered her suave words and caresses, her face and the proximity of her breath as he relived his night with her. Soon, her large eyes turned into more globous, vitreous eyes as the lovely face of his geisha shaped into the triangular head-capsule of a praying mantis, standing at the foot of his bed. At first, he ignored it as some avatar that his playful mind couldn't control.

'Scrunch, scrunch, scrunch …'

In the corridor, a slow shuffling of feet went past his door. An old woman was picking up empty plastic wraps lined with aluminum. She was ranting about the careless youth in a language incomprehensible to him. He turned over, his body fighting the vision of the insect as a lurid and unwelcomed sight. He heard the scrunch of the crisp foil in her old hand, his brain suddenly registering every sound acutely despite his deep sleep. The sound reverberated so loud in his head that he had to open his eyes, still asleep. As he raised his head above the sheets to check if the mantis was still there, a human-size triangular head with green round eyes was looking at him, expectant on his movements … A praying mantis, its slurping mandibles crunching slowly, its green globous eyes riveted on to his by means of two tiny fluorescent irises in the darkness of his room. Before he could distinguish the body attached to the head, he saw the muscular mandibles gnawing at his bed frame. As his eyes acclimatized better to the night, he suddenly looked at the Mantis with horror. It was still, frozen in predatory wakefulness. Poised, her forelegs toned, its three-fold arms prone, its mandibles toothed with razor-sharp barber's clippers, pumping with raw intensity. Her globulus green eyes now stared at him intensely as his own muscles tetanised in terror. Doherty thought at first that he was hallucinating. He meant to talk but his words remained stuck in his throat. He lied back down, turning around under his sheets, his hands pulling the white linen cover over his head in fear. He kept telling himself he was dreaming, when he opened his eyes again, but could only see the green glow of the mantis's eyes through the sheets. He had to surrender …He closed his eyes again, feeling his heart beating through his chest like a scared kid, listening to his heart pumping. He listened more intently for signs of the presence to go away. He believed for a moment that his ludircrous wishful thinking had worked. As he could not hear anything any more, he opened his eyes again. His mouth was dry. Too numb to move, he convinced himself that it was impossible that he saw what he saw, while his senses were overhwelmingly aware of the contrary, as he tried to lure his mind into a childish sense of security.

    Suddenly, he heard a loud chomp, as if a giant leaf was being torn apart in the dull emptiness of his room. In a vein attempt to laugh his vision off, he clasped the sheet, trying to convince himself that his brain was just regurgitating the memory of some intestinal rampage from last night. As he finally dared to look over the sheet, acutely aware of his delusion, he turned his head towards the foot of his bed and saw the same huge praying mantis manducating his legs, slupring with a deafening snarl, guzzling avidly on his flesh. Doherty inexplicably laughed with a snorting chuckle at first, in a desperate act of denial mixed with bravado, which turned into a nervous snicker, then a squeal, before he yelled for help in the darkness of the night. His will petrified. The mantis had hypnotised him, trapped him in denial, gaslighting his reason. His voice remained stuck in his throat but his laughter filled the room with deafening cruelty. As the laughter continued despite him, he kept convincing himself the whole nightmare was someone else's and that someone else was the butt of his joke.

In the corridor of the lodge, a few meters from Doherty's room, Jake thought he heard a noise in the night through the musical barrage of his headphones. He stopped the music and heard the slow shuffling of feet in the corridor. All he could hear was the groanings of an old woman, which made him smile. No need for translation, he figured. He knew all too well what the old lady was pestering against: fouling. She was picking up plastic packagings left by some uncivil youths, cursing the foulers' thoughtless act, her legs dragging her weight with difficulty on the floor carpet. He heard her steps receding when his opened eyes found the ondulating reflection of the blue waters of an exterior pond on the wall opposite his bed.

He watched the submerged pond lights reflection dancing on the walls. Stared vacantly at the rippling waves on the white canvas in front of him. In Jake's vision, the wall's surface was instinctively blurred by the gentle rolling lines of the pond waters. He switched the music back on. The vision and the sound were plesant enough. As a matter of fact, it was quite entrancing. He could give in to this delicious middle-of-the-night oblivion, feeling a sense a sleepiness overtaking him at last. He now sat motionless on the bed, his legs crossed and arms passively laid along his half-naked body, propped up by a couple of soft pillows.

He watched the blue-streaked moving lines of the water on the wall reflected by the hot springs lights dancing before his half-shut eyes, lulling him into deeper, calmer breathing; his eyes slowly shutting, when he saw a shape forming on the walls forcing his eyes open. It looked like a circle at first, a dark halo, which morphed into a larger circular black spot and whose inner circle was edged with sharp lighter edges, expanding to form a black hollow vacuum. In his hypnotic trance-like state, the ever-larger hole seemed to engulf the reflected ripples of water, forming what he thought was an eye, a human eye. But it wasn't. Instead, what he saw next was an enormous mouth sucking the light into a dark hole. Slosh, slosh, slosh … Suddenly, his music stopped and all he could hear was the sucking sound of a black hole which intimated him to stare and watch as the mouth became the mouth of a worm sucking the light into its intestinal system.

With a spasm of fear, he moved sideways on his bed to check if the vision was still there. He choked in the process. Caught his breath again as if the black hole meant to hoodwink him into diving deeper, so he would focus all his attention on the bewitching shape. Before he could fill his lungs with air, he saw a tunnel being formed by rings inside the open mouth. He felt as if the hole lined with incisive teeth was widening beyond the wall, but also coming ever closer towards him as it was expanding to the whole room, closer to him. His wide opened eyes now saw the mouth expanding to suck in his bed, his body feeling like a mere rubber toy, passively flexing to better enter the mouth. As he saw the sharp teeth of the mouth getting closer, he looked at this body and noticed with horror that it was already halfway inside while the sloshing sound continued louder and louder; a sound that had hypnotised him in the first place. He felt his numb body being sucked into the engulfing space and sliding towards its slimy rings, unavoidably gravitating towards its center, deeper towards the black hole inside, submerged by the moist and gooey feeling of a giant condom wrapped around his waist, irremediably siphoned into the warm intestines of the worm …In the early hours of the morning, outside the lodge, a vehicle parked with a squeaking of metal and clinking of glass. The driver got off, his boots clunking on the stoned pavement at the front of the lodge, removed some pallets piled up on the ground and shoved them into his trailer, then unloaded another pallet and covered it with tarpaulin. The delivery guy got back onto his truck and started the engine.

All Beatrice heard was the sound of the choke, then the engine turning over and sputtering before roaring away until it was faintly perceptible in the distance. Clank, clock, shrunk, clank, clock, shrunk … Now, she heard the faint sound of the distant engine blending with the dulled sound of the air conditioning fan blades rubbing intermittently against the fan's flanges.

Sprawled on the bed on her front, she removed the sheet covering her naked body with her toes, her arms now spread across the mattress in an easy and poetic hiatus between deep sleep and REM. Her firm buttocks glowing in the night, her nudity was exposed to the moonlit sky penetrating from the window, the hairs on her legs and thighs shining with blondness.

Her fingers started twitching effortlessly close to her head as if they were playing an iterative melody, practising scales. She breathed deeper, soothed by the sound of the air conditioning blades, and the pulsing distant swashing sound of the air sputtered by the fan. She felt a twitch in her groin, an involuntary muscle spasm that woke her up. She saw her fingers moving, as if animated by a force of their own: crawling, creeping, fawning beside her head. As she looked closer at her fingers, she saw the head of a spider moving swiftly from left to right and right to left as if to avoid her gaze. She let out a gasp, overtaken by fright. She quickly groped her way out of bed, using her arms and legs, but banged her thighs against the metallic bedside table.

As she stood up, vacillating, the sudden move made her whole body swerve under her own weight, as if a gravitational pull had destabilised her center of gravity. She ran towards the door where she saw herself clutch at the door handle and brush against the light switch in her fall. The room was fully lit now. She was being sucked into the intensity of a dream awash with light, when she saw the spider crawl over the bed towards her. She felt she had no choice but to surrender to an extraneous voice that intimated her there was nowhere else to go. She squealed so loudly that she opened her eyes again, clutching and clanking frantically at the knob on her bedside table, squinting at a fist-size spider crawling over her body. Then, she recognized the face of Jackson as the nightmarish spider's chelicerae gripped her abdominals and the pedipalp fumbled for a way inside her. She suddenly woke up to the hovering shadow of an arachnid magnified by the moon over her bedstead. Her face felt scratched and sore …

The Cleansing

Jake's dope-smoker's phlegmatic morning cough was soundless. He coughed several times intentionally, forcing the air out of his lungs to the point he nearly puked, in a desperate attempt to check if any sound would come out of his mouth, but his voice was mute. His head in a mash, the lodge already bustling with activity at breakfast was full of sounds however. He could hear echos in the hall, the rumour from the corridors, the usual morning sounds of a hotel waking up to the light of day. But when Jake tried to say a few words outloud, no sound came out of his mouth despite feeling his throat vibrating. He rushed to the bathroom mirror to see if he still had a face. He looked at his Adam's apple, it was more prominent than usual. He felt for it, but it bounced under his fingers like a plunger under water.

He freaked out. As he decided his muteness had to be associated with some sort of curse, a spell cast to punish him, still facing the mirror, he remembered howling abuse at Mr. Hashita. Was he now paying for his insolence?

Fortunately for him, the breakfast guests were equally quiet around the table. He wasn't the odd-one out this time, as the restaurant was empty, save for a couple of elderly people sitting romantically at a table in the garden where a large aloe vera plant was shining in the sun. The man, a westerner, was dressed in a grey tuxedo and the woman, a Japanese lady, was wearing a night dress. Jake found the whole scene incongruous but anything was possible after the vision he had had during the night.

- 'Are you okay, Jake?'

Jake shook his head. He noticed Beatrice behind him.

- 'Just tell me, what is it?'

Jake pointed to his throat and wagged his finger.

- 'We're in that mood, hey?' said Beatrice.

No matter what his frantic eyes and gestures tried to tell her, she couldn't possibly know he was mute. He gave up trying to tell anyone about his manifest predicament.

Their hotel and other hotels in the area had been told to close their doors. An emergency hotel for tourists would be open soon, but no location had been decided yet, according to the hotel manager, a paperthin Chinese man who stood vicariously by their table and whose red cheeks were lit by a large smile. Behind the strangely dressed couple, beyond the garden, down the isle where all bedrooms face the hills, hot springs and the mountain range beyond, the smoke at the surface of the water could be seen writhing up in the moist-laden air, between fennel plants and indolent Camellias. At the bar, the sleepy buxom waitress in a white shirt and black skirt was gawping at the spurting clunky coffee machine. Doherty arrived at the only dressed table in the cafeteria. He looked at the waitress, bemused, and sat down, dragging his chair with gravitas. He was followed by Jonathan who sat silently, wishing good morning to no one. Hashita was already sat, inconscpicuously ignorant of the world around him. His eyes closed. Beatrice looked embarrassed, hesitant to come forward with the night's ghouly harvest:

- 'I had a terrible nightmare last night! I don't know what to make of it,' she said with humility, cutting through the silent atmosphere with her spoon.
- 'You too?' said Doherty, staring at her with globous eyes, peering into her face with interest.
  'You have marks on your face, Beatrice, what happened to you?' he asked.
- 'Oh, it's nothing, nothing like it was this morning when I woke up anyway. I must have scratched myself during my sleep. But it's healing fast, I think!' she said.

She looked at her reflection in her phone, pleased with the progress of scarification.

- 'Oh, no, you can see them still!' exclaimed Jonathan, agasp, as if his reaction had been delayed. 'Show me,' he said, holding her arm forcefully.
- 'Jake couldn't talk this morning. Monk Hashita touched his knee yesterday,' said Beatrice, anxious.
- 'Did he now?' Jonathan posed, suddenly erect on his seat, like an alert squirrel, looking around the room for danger.

Jake observed through narrowed eyes at Deadstone's strange behaviour, then glanced reproachfully at Hashita:

- 'Hashita san, is this true?' asked Jonathan, exaggeratedly indignant.

The monk muttered a few words in Japanese and then cleared his throat:

- 'It was nothing, really. Just innocent chat with Jake.'

He stared in the distance, his little beady eyes as sharp as knives.

- 'You crazy, walking out on me like that?'

He glanced at Jake deprecatingly.

- 'Probably overblown, hey Jake?' Jonathan commented captiously.
- 'Please, apologize!' the monk suddenly shouted in his peremptory and martial Japanese accent. Anyone around the table had to conclude his honour had been hurt irreparably. All were expectant on each other to speak ...

The table remained silent however. Jonathan was adamant Jake should account for his behaviour:

- 'You must be strong before flower, even dreams must be strong! Dreams are first stage of cleansing,' said Hashita peremptorily.

Hashita bowed his head and fell silent himself.

- 'So, Jake? What do you have to say for your defence? The man is ensuring our safety, and you insult him?' said Jonathan, reproachfully.

But Jake was mute. No words would come out of his mouth when he tried to speak. Instead, he stared at the monk, his eyes seething with bottled up anger.

- 'Er … My dream last night was quite terrible, actually,' said Beatrice, meekly.

Doherty butted in with an offbeat swaggering joke.

- 'I had to grapple with a six-foot tall manga mantis during the night, she had lovely green eyes but ate my legs,' he said, ogling at the yassified barista behind the bar.
- 'This isn't the time nor the place, Roger, the kids obviously had a terrible night. Look at Beatrice and Jake, they are distraught,' said Jonathan, disparagingly.
- 'Okay, okay, well, so am I,' blurted Doherty, tapping his nails on the corner of the Formica-covered table.
- 'Let's hear it! Beatrice first,' said Jonathan, emphatically.

As she heard the bell, the waitress finally shook off her apathetic morning torpor and came serving the breakfast at their table. Doherty came out of his to try and attract her attention. She brought green balls of sticky bean paste, long soft and squidgy octopus limbs, some milky corn soup to their table.

- 'What a lovely country Japan is, I am under its charm,' said Doherty, leering at the waitress's cleavage.
- 'Hotel open especially for you,' she said, 'because Covid'.
- 'Excuse me,' asked Beatrice, 'Who are these elderly people over there?'
- 'Oh!' Mr. and Mrs. Pox, always here this time of year, to celebrate spring. Mrs. Pox, a dancer,' said the glum waitress.
- 'You can tell,' commented Jonathan. 'The straight lines of the elderly lady's torso and her muscular toned back seemed to have told may times the story of movement beautifully' he continued, while the guests around the table gasped at the couple's incongruous evening clothes.

- Are they dead?' asked Jonathan.

They all looked at the elderly couple, looking at each other in silence, smiling: a still image in the glorious morning mountain sun coming through the garden … Jake noticed a tattoo between the woman's shoulder blades: a flower, a blue flower with radiating lines blending with the tone of her pale white skin.

The breakfast chat proved to be cathartic and liberating after all. Jake couldn't believe his own ears. They all came out with the truth, exposing their vulnerability and weaknesses, defoliated, bare, as if nothing could stop them from spewing out their blinding secrets or unabashed revelations. Even, the monk finally turned to Jake and apologized about his pulsion towards him. He had meant nothing untoward but to show a little affection towards Jake. He reverted smoothly into his gentle self as Doherty burst into tears, shamed by his lustful conduct, quickly redeemed by the rest of the group who comforted him at the table. Doherty, for that matters, came clean on his real mission on Mount Asahi: him and Taylor were member of a cult founded by Master Khul, a blind monk whose visions had heralded a female prophet. They had plans to spread it to the western world and Beatrice had been chosen as their messiah. Beatrice listened to Doherty, nonplussed. Jonathan, who had not quite been able to figure out Doherty since the beginning of the expedition, was equally dumbfounded. He emulated Doherty and broke down into tears too, admitting his grief had made him bitter and thankful for the love he felt towards Beatrice, whom he had nevertheless been stalking. Beatrice, who was no exception to the terrible rule of the cleansing that preceded the flower's ceremony, had been repressing her love for her mother because of her father's death, which she blamed her for. She had been flirtatious with her uncle whom she knew was in love with her.

Jake was told to move the expedition pack to the front of the lodge, as an act of contrition. He protested but couldn't argue his case. Before leaving the table, Hashita glanced at Jake lewdly and smiled:

- 'Keep an open mind,' he said. 'Flower speaks many tongues.'

While the expedition members were gathering in the German-themed lobby of the lodge in anticipation of his advice for the next leg of the journey, the buxom waitress came running towards them. Jake saw her enormous breast bouncing in a figure of eight under her shirt. She chortled and said:

- 'Mr. Deadstone-san?
- Yes?
- Air ambulance called, they found your friend! Please call them now,' she said, her face radiating with the good news.
- 'Oh, thank you. That's a relief, thanks a lot, and sayonara!' said Jonathan, lost for words.

He bowed ceremoniously. He took the number she had written on a napkin and walked outside to call the air ambulance:

- 'Hi, may I speak to the …Oh, yes, you're the English expedition on Mount Asahi? Please wait.
- Er … Hullo? I am Jonathan Deadstone, do you speak English? Do you have a message for me?
- Oh, yes, let me pass you on to the doctor who examined your friend. Just a minute.
- Dr. Yamahista, speaking, how may I help?
- I am Dr. Deadstone, my friend, Mr. Dubois died on the mountain …
- Oh, yes. Hmmm … Right. Yes, it seems that we have found a strange case of worms in the body.
- Worms, you say?
- Yes, in three days, the worms have unfortunately eaten half of the body's organs.
- What kind of worms?
- The flesh-eating type,' said the doctor.

Jonathan looked at his arm. The bulge had grown overnight. He instantly made the connection with the itch and the bloating he had been feeling for the past few days. He felt drops of sweat pearl on his forehead. The worm larvae had to be extracted as soon as possible.

As for Beatrice, this morning felt like slipping into a different skin. She pried on the couple dressed up to the nines in the restaurant's garden. She waved at them. They waved back. She walked over to the table and said 'hi,' but the couple were strangely surrounded by a bubble of aloofness that she felt she couldn't penetrate. She thought she heard a song:

Fennel and Orange.

People walking past.

Some slow and some fast.

She now felt a sense of completion, as if last night's rite of passage had sassified her. She felt stronger. Jonathan took her to the higher garden for a chat:

- 'Are you alright?' said Jonathan.
- 'I couldn't believe it was a hallucination … It was so real!' said Beatrice.
- 'When I heard that laughter that night, I couldn't believe it either at first.
- What is it do you think, Unk?
- Collective hallucination,' said Jonathan.
- 'How is that possible?
- Have I told you the story of that girls school in Japan who went on a field trip to the forest and all fainted at once?
- All of them?
- All of them fell asleep in the forest and woke up not knowing what had happened … So we all faced our worst nightmares to become stronger, is that it?
- So it seems …
- Unk, am I really the chosen one?' asked Beatrice, unpretendingly, 'Are my dreams connected to the flower?
- They are, but they are not synchronised yet. Don't let this dream-state fool you, it usually precedes a coming-of-age ceremony that may cancel its magic. Don't you underestimate the magic either. Remember the mind is an illusion …
- It's strange, it's exactly what Jake said on the plane. I am worried about him. He hasn't said a word since this morning,' said Beatrice, 'I am not sure what the monk has in store for him.
- We shall see soon enough. As for I, I am beginning to think that Doherty is the one to watch out for. Him and his snowballing cult are about to be put to the test, believe you me!'

Jonathan laughed heartedly, letting the expeditionists' cleansing fall into his lap as a blessing, happy that it wasn't his job to interpret or interfere with their dreams. In front of the lodge, after breakfast, Boula, their sherpa bundled Jake's equipment. Boula was from the Mugu district in Nepal. He had been hired by Dubois. He smiled, revealing his pearly white teeth, against his bronze UVB tan. He was greeted by the group.

- 'Dubois hired him a long time ago. He's been staying with friends, waiting for this expedition all this time,' said the monk, translating for him.

Boula was shorter than the rest of them. He was dressed in a parka, wearing a bandana around his head. His carved triangular face and emaciated traits testified to his seasoned experience of high-altitude expeditions.

They walked up to the tree line. The ascent took five hours. Hashita stopped on a plateau where a coppice of one-sided trees provided a shelter against the freezing northwesterly winds. He stood in front of the group, his long traditional green monk robe flapping in the wind. Beatrice glanced at the sherpa's handmade leather shoes. She compared her walking boots and then Jake's. She had not had time to talk to him about his feelings. She looked at Jake's shoes with empathy.

- 'Everybody, please listen! It's noon and we late. Please make sure you open eyes and ears to each other. Stay silent when we arrive at camp, it's important you listen to your heart, and be aware. Now, let's meditate as taught by Master Khul. You need find inner silence before you can enter flower territory. Please, practice!' said Hashita.

Hashita crouched and sat down on the flaps of his long open Safran windproof fleece, opened on a jaded green Shinto monk robe, which impressed the group who marvelled at its long golden-laced threads. On his chest and neck were printed multicoloured tattooed flowers and Japanese characters. A pink camellia or a peony on his chest, Beatrice couldn't quite tell, was framed in a quadratic circle. She was particularly impressed with the tattoos.

- 'First, please breathe and connect to your body, experience the air flowing around your limbs. Breathe naturally, deeply … And close your eyes. Let the air move inside. Let it tell you the story of your body. Listen to that story. The breaks, the bruises, the scars, the hurt, the joys, the pleasures and the rest. Focus on every part, from your toes, feet, ankles, knees to crutch, groin, waist, belly, stomach, plexus, shoulders, neck and head. Breathe in, breathe out, that's right. Slowly … Patiently. Listen to the air move around. What does it say about your body?' the monk chanted.

Hashita felt the wave of feelings coming from the group, mindful of their presence and energy, he accompanied their breathing for a few minutes, breathing with them, individualising what everyone already knew but might have forgotten …

- 'Now, if you are ready, say those words: "I have this body but I am more than this body," out loud, if you want or inside, as you wish … '

Stirring the spiritual pot within the group, Hahista kept an eye on Jake who had just opened his eyes. He saw the monk looking at him. He glanced at his tattoos and shut his eyes again, abidingly …

- 'Now, please continue breathing deeply. What are your feelings, please investigate. Maybe unsure, maybe excited, maybe angry, who knows? Focus on your breathing, what do you feel? Where are those feelings in your body?' said Hashita.

They were all breathing loudly now, their eyes closed, the wild rising wind around them singing in unison with their breath.

- 'Breathe in, breathe out,' said Hashita monotonously, alternating between silent pauses and guiding words.

  - 'Now, when ready, say those words: "these are my feelings, but I am more than these feelings".'

Hashita took a deep breath and poised, listening to the group's collecting breathing rhythm.

- 'Focus on your thoughts now. What am I thinking inside, what are my thoughts made of? Please, investigate your thoughts, but please breathe deeply, regularly … That's right.'

Again, a few seconds passed, and the group was stirred by a wave of self-knowledge. Thoughts seemed printed on their forehead. Hashita could read them like open books.

- 'And now, when you're ready, say those words: "I am these thoughts, but I am more than these thoughts".'

The peaceful group abided silently, forming one single mass of matter swayed by a common current of primeval thought. Doherty mumbled the words out loud. All eyes were still closed. Hashita took a deep breath and said:

- 'And now, if you are ready, say those words: "I am a pure centre of consciousness and will".'

He observed the group, bent forward, head bowed, muttering the words he had told them to repeat, and thought satisfyingly that the warning the night before might have been powerful enough to hoodwink them into the trap he had layed for them …

Angels of Lies

A tribute. A sound that no one hears ... The camp lay still in the dead of night, where spirits, free to roam, invest dreams with ease. Some have left the key to their soul on the door of their consciousness. Some have suffered so much that the pain is everlastingly entangled in history with essences of beings lost or robbed from earthly desires ...Tonight would be the last blooming night of the Everblue. They all braved the warnings and the hurt of their finite haikus of life only to discover their universe was not to last beyond their dreams. But in the morning, each and everyone would be facing the Everblue's implacable revelation: the fickle truth of their existence in the grand scheme of things. They crossed the Rubicon without noticing, strained by the altitude, sore from the forced march, dulled by the cold.

Tonight, Hashita would retire from his life of meditation. Guiding the last pilgrims around the peaks of his native land, he hoped to serve the purpose of his life one last time before he laid down his weapon at the mouth of the sacred cave harbouring the Everblue. His job was to open hearts to the beauty of life in acceptance of death, the material burden of proof everyone faces one day or another. As a guide, his mission was to take his disciples through the hierarchy of lies that plagued the human race since its beginning. Each and every tribe or society he guided usually built the present upon the past and the future upon what they know to be true. But the spiritual circles of his journey into the souls of human beings had always led him to this moment of reckoning before the flower. This time, he only had to answer one relentless question: had he honoured his divine duty and his vows to the best of his ability?

From the young age of twenty-one, he had learnt suffering and rebirth, and where did that get him exactly? As a Shinto monk, he was supposed to serve humanity and connect the dots of lives entangled in the universal breath. To find harmony between the elements: water, air and earth, he had learnt to become sentient of their part in the human story and to withdraw from their presence.

This knowledge, latent in every breath and sinew, had grown. But he knew they were fickle parts of the wider dream the flower initiated its pilgrims to.

He never looked back on his vows with regret, but tonight was particularly full of doubt. He knew this would be his last expedition. He had shared his qualms with Dubois and Master Khul. Master Khul had said '*The path to enlightenment needs no light.*' He had pondered his advice with great poise and respect, but had not found it particularly helpful. Now, however, as the last night of his terrestrial existence doomed upon him, he took the blade out of the scabbard ... Well-hidden from sight, on his back, the swishing sound of the blade instantly reminded him of his Yakuza youth. The first time he used it was the moment he had tried to forget all his life. A poor bugger who had defected from the ranks, his indebtment to the ruthless organisation, and his *yubitsume*, which had been ordered and suffered no delay. He knew he would lose more than a finger if he didn't comply.

Instead of honouring his assignment, he had hidden from his *kyodai*, his big brother in the organisation, during his tenure in the very heartland of Yakuzas, the island of Kyushu. But the metropolitan police also had their fingers in the pie and intended to claim the prize of his freedom as part of their arrangement with the criminal organisation. He had been commissioned to kill the renegade. Hashita had been staking him, following orders from the *Wakagashira*, the first lieutenant. But Hashita, against his orders, had given him his freedom back and told him to hide in a Buddhist monastery.

His blade was his witness. He carried it everywhere the order of his monkhood had led him while he hid from the organisation. 'A personal gift' he told anyone who asked int the way of an excuse for carrying such a weapon to the places he travelled across the region. But Hashita knew it was no gift. It was a curse that would never leave him.

Now, in his tent, in the middle of Mount Asahi's total tranquility, he could feel the cold invading his couch, his blade lying beside him. If he had to use it again—as he knew he would as soon as the flower performed its dark magic on his guests—he would have to break his vows and his mission would be over. The blade would sever the thread of his wandering life. He spent the rest of the night lying his head outside his tent, gazing at the milky way and stars whizzing in the vault of ancient dreams. Stones had been gathered to protect the fire. The flower was a mile away, he had told the guests. Jonathan had requested that the monk showed him the flower before the rest of them, to make sure there was no danger.

How could he ask for a rehearsal? Hashita had sneered at his request for a sneak preview of the flower. The trip to see the Everblue was a unique experience, he had told Deadstone. How could he ask for such a favour? Hashita knew that facing the flower would be the last Jonathan would see of Beatrice too. It was meant to be that way and just like "love at first sight", he explained to Jonathan, presentation to the flower couldn't be rehearsed.

Master Khul had told him how the flower knew no bounds, but that his ancestral mettle had prepared him all his life. Still, Master Khul, had shown him how to approach it, with emptiness, bareness and sincerity, trusting in the universal truth of nothingness. Hashita was the guide in charge now since the Yakuzas had caught up with Khul. What did it mean, had he pondered for months, what on earth did that mean? How does on interpret "nothingness"? He remembered the words of the late Master Khul, as he fetched the wood logs the sherpa had deposited near his tent.

'The path to inner silence is the end of all dreams.'

Master Khul had warned him against his own state of awakening in the material world.

'It is useless to think one can think alone on this earth. No spirit would allow it.'

The path was the path, he had thought. Master Khul had lost his to find the flower. Did that mean it was the path of the lost ones?

After the forced nap imposed by Hashita as a prerequisite to the last ceremony, Jake was the first to come out of his tent. He saw the fire and the monk pouring his spirit over the flames as if he was talking to them. He walked slowly towards him and smiled. The monk greeted him with a nod. Jake sat down and opened his parka's pocket, handed a bar of chocolate to the monk who waved as if to say "no need". Jake felt ashamed. The monk looked at him and nodded again. Jake returned his nod. He had been forgiven. Now was the time for the monk to forgive himself, seemed to chant the universe.

Hashita lifted his head to the morning sky and cried. All the while, a prescient feeling kept nagging Beatrice whose individual knowledge of life was full of the bountifulness and generosity of her predestined motherhood. They weren't alone. During the night, she had felt a creeping presence around the tents. Hashita had told them about the visions they would encounter during their ascent journey.

'*They are common at night, but more so during the day,*' he had told them.

He had warned them about the spirits guarding the flower, the "Yōkai" Master Khul and Dubois already knew about, because the spirit could take the shape of a known creature, often, between monkey and bird of prey; a monkey with wings being among the most common sights. Beatrice had not felt her tent had been visited by a monkey but rather by a human figure …The tea pot was now hot, so everyone gathered around the fire, waiting on Hashita to speak some incantations before the final push. Silence had to be observed without compromise, he had said.

Now, it was time for the spirits to show themselves. As the legend predicted, each of them would be severed from their human bond with the group, but in spirit, they could always find themselves and each other if they had the force and the will to do so. Hence the silence, had explained Hashita.

Beatrice brushed against Jake, sitting beside him by the fire. She drank the tea Hashita had prepared. It was now or never, intimated Jake, handing Beatrice a steaming cup. She could pretend, but it was her choice.

Jonathan reserved his judgment about the whole procedure as he had not seen any spirit the night before, but he observed the silence anyhow, conscious not to challenge Hashita's sense of duty. The Everblue would be inviting the members of the expedition soon enough, had said Hashita. Jonathan scrutinised studiously his every move. Jake seemed to have a place of honour at his side, he noticed, while Doherty ambled around the fire, stretching his legs, carefully avoiding making a sound.

The conflagration of inner silence can be a terrible ordeal for those who are not used to it, had warned Hashita. He had reserved his judgment as to Jake's abilities, now he looked at Jonathan and Doherty as the weakest links. '*Those men have no control over their thoughts,*' had predicted Master Khul, who knew Dubois to be one of them. '*Sit a few men around a fire, and none of them will shut up,*' had said Master Khul, waving his moralist finger in the air. Hashita could feel it now, the talking monkeys found it hard to stop the flow of their thoughts as they spurted through the silence of creation. He had seen it all before. Men betrayed their destiny with their mouth, carving the domain of reality with their science. Two men of science such as them would deny the very existence of the Everblue until they had seen it, had warned Master Khul. But Hashita explained to them, following the meditation, that the Everblue had a spirit of its own and that it required acceptance of them rather than the other way round. Beatrice smiled at the sight of her uncle being condemned to silence. Jake had taken surprisingly quickly to the precept, taking it in his stride. He had been prepared since the hotel.

Now was the moment of untruth. As the lights of the milky way disappeared over the camp carved in the flank of the mountain and the sun appeared in the horizon, Hashita rose to his feet and held a bowl in his hand:

- 'This is the bowl of incantation. Listen to its sound,' said Hashita solemnly.

The expeditionists listened to the eery dirge that emanated from the sounding bowl. They all stood alert, some in fear of retribution, some puzzled. Before long, Hashita saw Jake sprang to his feet and gesticulate wildly to protect himself from invisible demons that were threatening to enter his ears. Hashita saw him vacillate, tripping over and fall head first on a rock. Jake fell unconscious. Meanwhile, Beatrice gawped in horror at the sight of flying monkeys, half-macaques, half-hawks, hovering around her head, trying to snatch and clutch at her hair. Hashita watched the napping girl fight the invisible spirits off in her trance, as she lied on the ground, dreaming. Hashita nodded. He couldn't see them but knew Beatrice had been chosen by the Yōkai. He recognised the beasts' flying patterns by observing Beatrice's movements. He knew they were taking her spirit away.

On the other side of the camp, Doherty was battling with yet another mirage of a green-eyed mantis whose forelegs were slashing at his stomach, as he was seen running around the camp, trying to fight the giant insect off, throwing stones at the monstrous silhouette. Hashita watched him punch his own stomach!

Hashita looked at them all, like a civil servant presiding over a tribunal, imbued with a stately sense of duty and conscientiousness. He saw Jonathan hurrying towards a precipice. He observed how he contemplated the void before jumping deliberately into a crevice to protect himself from his invisible attacker. To Jonathan, it was a dragon whose flames were now burning his groin.

Master Khul had warned him this would happen. Their hallucinations had better not be arrested or the flower would fade and die. It was part of the deal, Master Khul had said.

'They need to confront their fears, so their fear cannot confront them.'

The sherpa was strangely quiet, observing the monk and witnessing their hallucinations. But even this subservient observer soon started running up and down the hill as if he was chased by his own shadow. Hashita knew that, within a few hours, they would all be extenuated and sore from their dreams. The day was going to be long. They would tire themselves out and then, in the evening, he would take them to the flower.

Had Dubois been here, reflected the monk, he would have interfered with the prophecy of the Everblue. As a man of science, he would have asked questions, tried to elucidate meaning, ask everyone about their dream, taking notes. Hashita had protected the prophecy, as he was bound to by virtue of the allegiance he had sworn to Master Khul and the cult of the Everblue …

Acceptance

Except for the rising winds on top of Asahi mount, the Japanese spring setting sun lulled the party into a sweet sense of tranquillity ... Most of the initiated ones were still asleep. Hashita had dressed up formally: his Shinto purified robe, the Kariginu, an ochre garb with broad sleeves with overlapping neckband neatly tucked under his saffron fleece. He was also wearing his traditional coif, a beige paper-wood-lacquer Kanmuri hat. The octagonal patterns of his garment were encrusted with embroidered schematic flowers. He stood arms akimbo, pondering the void under them. Dark ominous twilight clouds with silver linings had gathered in the valley below.

Jonathan woke up from his daymare, some twenty yards from the top of the plateau where Beatrice was still asleep. Doherty and Jake soon rose from their slumber quasi simultaneously. They found the monk reciting some incantations in his native language. Hashita's hypnotic chants had reached Jonathan's ears down the crevice. Doherty threw him a rope mechanically. Every move seemed stage-managed by an invisible orchestrator who had given each one a task. Jonathan tied the rope around his waist. Once he was hoisted to safety, they checked his injuries.

- 'You'll be fine. You look like a monk now,' said Doherty, referring to the rope around his waist.
- 'Aye, but not a Buddhist one! What on earth happened? It felt like an exorcism. I think I have a cracked rib. Damn, are we even allowed to speak now?'

The camp fire was now glowing in the dusk.

- 'It is time now,' said Hashita. 'You've all been cleansed. There's no going back now!'

He choked the fire.

- 'Can I talk now?' asked Jake, combing Beatrice's hair with her folding comb. Beatrice had just woken up too, visibly groggy after her fight against imaginary monsters.
- 'We'll talk about dreams later,' said Hashita, marshalling the group towards him.

They all look at Hashita's robe and dignified posture, his hands tucked under his strapping belt.

- 'What about my uncle's cracked rib, Mr. Hashita?' asked Beatrice, her head still muzzy.
- 'Oh, he'll be fine,' said Jonathan, "self-soothing".

Hashita nodded.

- 'Talking is okay now. But hurry, we must leave soon.
- Jonathan san, everything okay?' asked Hashita.
- 'I'm fine, just a big bruise, I think. I'll go and get some moss!'

Hashita sighed.

- 'But quick. Flower will not wait.'

Jonathan picked some sphagnum moss, which he knew worked on open wounds and also some yarrow and witch-hazel, to speed up healing. He munched the plants and applied them in a poultice under a makeshift bandage on his ribs.

- 'Wow, cool, Unk,' said Beatrice, amazed at his presence of mind.
- 'It helps knowing about herbs,' said Hashita. 'When I was a monk, we grew garden herbs. Holy basil you might need now, to finish cleansing.
- Sure,' said Jonathan, 'or night goggles.'
- 'Hashita says to hurry,' said Doherty snivellingly, standing firmly on his two feet, his rucksack on his back, standing by Hashita's side, like the jewel in the crown.

The expedition party got ready for the last ascension. Doherty switched on his headlamp and followed Hashita as they climbed towards the top of the rock face that lead to a higher plateau.

- 'It's this way, Jake,' said Beatrice.
- 'We can talk now,' said Jake, 'what was your daymare about?'
- 'I just can't remember, can you?'
- 'No, it's just my head hurts,' said Jake.
- 'Unk!' shouted Beatrice, 'Jake might need some of that moss for his head!'

Jonathan stopped in his track behind Doherty before climbing the dripping snaky trail winding between rocks.

- 'Just give me a minute,' said Jonathan.

He fumbled for some moss in his bag, but could find none.

- 'Here, take some of mine,' he said, removing some of the poultice from the bandage he had used for his ribs.
- 'How does it feel, Unk?' asked Beatrice.
- 'Not too bad, I feel it's working already. But this damn skin hitch is getting worse,' said Jonathan.
- 'I thought you'd attended to it,' said Beatrice.
- 'I did, but I couldn't extract every single larvae. The flies must have laid eggs everywhere,' said Jonathan.

Jonathan hesitated before applying the healing herb to Jake's head, pausing for a second.

- 'Are you sure you're okay Unk?' said Beatrice, worried.
- 'Oh, I ... I'm just wondering if exchanging fluids is hygienic. But there's no time to get some more moss, and there's no choice, he needs a bandage,' said Jonathan.

His fingers moved mechanically, wrapping the bandage around Jake's head.

- 'Just a small contusion, Jake, you should be fine. Remove it when your head stops hurting.
- Er … Okay,' Jake looked at him, perplexed.
- 'Deadstone, we need to go now!' shouted Doherty.

They looked up at him, arms akimbo, his face dripping with sweat, panting for breath at the top of the rock face, posing as the leader's sidekick.

- 'We need to get a move on, now,' shouted Hashita from his promontory. 'Time is of the essence!
- Albright, alright. You go first, Bee. Not you Jake,' said Jonathan.

Jonathan followed Beatrice and Jake found himself at the end of the rope. The sherpa stayed behind to guard the camp. After an hour or so, once they had climbed a sharp outcrop streaming with rain and melting snow, the party reached the nimb of the mountain. Hashita showed them the entrance of the grotto where he meant to give one last incantation before presenting the group to the flower. And here it was indeed, a few meters ahead of them, just as Hashita had described it. They could see another misty outcrop where a glowing blue iridescence signalled its presence. It was night now, the moon soon disappeared behind the clouds and there was no light except the fluorescent entrails of the grotto where Hashita removed his outer clothes layer and asked everyone to do the same:

- 'What? Are you crazy, in this cold?' Beatrice whispered to Jake.

Hashita admonished her with a dark glance that Jonathan disapproved at first, but felt under the obligation to agree to, placing his fatherly hand on Beatrice's shoulder to steady her. Their heart beating, the party observed Hashita and imitated him. Beatrice whispered:

- 'I can't take off my top, it's freezing.
- Do it over there behind the rocks, won't you? Go quickly! The flower is right there!' supplicated Jonathan.

The magnetic field around the grotto felt palpable now. Beatrice felt her tousled hair with her hands. It was crackling with electricity. She walked towards a granite outcrop and removed her parka, then her sweater, but stopped short of the thermal on her upper body. She saw the party disappear into the mouth of the cave one by one, except for Jake and Jonathan.

As she looked back down at the trail, she saw a silhouette coming towards her fast, as if the stranger was making a bee line for her. She gasped. Taylor had been following the expeditionists and was intent on grabbing hold of her. She saw his berserk wild eyes honing on her. She waited for a word, an explanation, but instead he snatched a rock and struck her head. He then dragged her unconscious body towards the trail, lifting it to his shoulders, then strapped her around his neck and upper arms like a deer.

As Beatrice didn't return, Hashita summoned the whole group one last time in the mouth of the grotto with their bare chest, as instructed. Jonathan protested at first, but Hashita reminded him that it was now or never. His tattoos had raised suspicion with Jake who had stayed at the back of the group, attentive and alert, fearful. But Hashita was pressing them on, arguing that the blue glow could disappear at any moment now, that the flower would sleep for another year once the glow faded. Jake hesitated before stepping into the cave, looking over his shoulder, peering into the night for any sign Beatrice was following them …

- 'It's now or never, Jonathan san. We can't wait for the girl!' said Hashita.

Jonathan looked back and shouted Beatrice's name, but he had a feeling that she might not want to remove her top and would see them all later, when they heroically morph into supernatural beings on their return or something similarly extraordinary. Jonathan Deadstone didn't know what to think. He procrastinated but entered the grotto. They all pussyfooted towards the blue effervescence with electric anticipation: Hashita first, then Doherty, followed by Jonathan and Jake, who had waited for Jonathan to walk in front of him. Soon, Jake lost his hearing. He wasn't able to heed Jonathan's warning about the blade glowing in the dark, under the blue gleaming luminescence of the flower. Jake saw the blade skewer the air but couldn't see who was holding the blade.

He saw the monk's face clearly now that Hashita suddenly lunged at Doherty. Hashita was jubilant, his eyes red with rage and glowing with frenetic mania. Jonathan rushed deeper inside the darkest bowels of the cave as he heard a body fall to the ground. Jake was petrified. Hashita was making for him now, his face was tense with homicidal intent, his body prone for attack. Jonathan crouched, terrified, expecting his turn any minute now, ready to reach back to the entrance of the cave in case he was discovered in the darkness. It was everyman for himself. Without thinking twice, Jonathan unexpectedly ran towards danger and the flower, enraptured, disregarding the threat even if he could be next as Doherty's head rolled down with a loud thump on the soil. He stepped towards the alcove where the flower was glowing in the dark. It now stood proudly before him. Five petals, a glowing orange center with red stamens haloed in a blue aura. Writhed around the stem, a giant red snake was predating on Jonathan's every move, following the movement of his head. Jonathan stood still, watching his flared nostrils, deaf to the cries of Jake whose tearful howls he could hear faintly. Jonathan was hypnotised by the snake and didn't see anything happening behind his back where the ominous shadow of death was lurking. He felt it on his neck however, breathing like a hungry beast ready to break his spine with its jaws. But Jonathan was obnubilated by the ovary, the pistils and the calice before his eyes. He didn't see Jake turning the blade against Hashita, after a flurry of blows that dumbed the monk. He didn't see him clutch the blade with his bare lacerated hands and snatch it from the monk to thrust his own demented vengeance into his heart, as if he had been trained all his life to slain the dragon!

Jonathan suddenly withdrew from his enthralling sight, or was made to, who could tell? But suddenly, he was holding his chest with both hands, trying to recover his breath, panting on the ground outside the grotto. Jake had resuscitated him. He felt the pain in his chest and gasped, struggling to recover his sight.

- 'You're back!' shouted Jake. 'You're back!'

Jonathan was catching his breath slowly, wheezing, trying to speak:

- 'Don't speak, Jonathan.
- Wh … ?
- Don't, it might kill you … Shut up!' said Jake.

Jonathan painstakingly raised his upper body on his elbows, looking into Jake's eyes.
- 'Where is B … ?' Jonathan floundered haltingly.
- 'She's fine. She's fine,' said Jake reassuringly.

Jonathan lost consciousness again. Thankfully breathing still, checked Jake. Jake stood up from his crouching position slowly, taking his fingers off Jonathan's pulse, and looked around but saw no signs of life coming out of the grotto. The blue iridescent glow had now turned into a flimsy shimmer of opalescence. He walked towards the cave and tripped over the body of Hashita, still breathing. The monk was lying with his wakiszshi blade by his side, in his left hand, the red saya exposed under his shinto robe. Jake listened on his breathing for a second until a terrible sense of danger forced him to his feet again. He saw Doherty's severed head, turned upside down, his trunk sputtering the last drops of blood left in his arteries, as his decaptiated body lay flat on his front, a few yards beyond. Jake suddenly realised with horror what had happened. The cave reeked of iron and fresh oozing blood. He walked towards Hashita, looking around the grotto for any sign of activity. But only the monk was humming, choking on his own blood:

- 'Why? Why, monk? Who are you? Are you even a monk, you motherfucker?' said Jake.

Jake felt his hands smarting. He was bleeding badly. He snatched a piece of the monk's robe, holding it diown with his foot, and tore it off to bandage his hands. The monk looked at him and smiled with a sardonic rictus that mutated into a grimace as he came round to Jake's standing next to him.

He looked down at Hashita, halting with a sneer on his face. Jake looked at him with disdain, pondering whether to finish him off with a rock or his own sword. He grabbed a large stone lying by the monk's flank, irresolute:

- 'Say it, you asshole, you Yakuza bastard!'

The monk was shaking his head dolefully, as if he meant that Jake couldn't possibly understand. Hashita took a few more short breaths …

- 'It feels … so good … ' said Hashita with arrogance.

Jake felt his fingers wrap around the rock with might, waiting for Hashita to ask for mercy. But Hashita mustered all his energy:

- 'Thank you,' he said.

Hashita was panting louder now, his eyes open-wide, looking at the ceiling of the grotto, as if he was seeing something unusual. A vision maybe. Hashita's rounded eyes stared intensely at the ceiling. Jake crouched, holding the rock with both hands. Hashita was dead.

Jake dropped the rock. He looked in the direction of the flower. It was frozen. He then looked up towards the ceiling of the cave following Hashita's last look and saw nothing. He ran outside to check on Jonathan, who was still unconscious. He felt for a sign of life again. Jonathan was alive but his pulse was weak. He went back to fetch Doherty's parka and covered Jonathan with it. Jonathan opened his eyes slowly:

- 'Thank you,' he whispered before falling unconscious again.

Jake looked around for any sign of Beatrice, shouted her name, but he couldn't leave Jonathan, not now …

Six Months After the Expedition

The fires of Samhuinn could be seen whirling in the air, passing swiftly in front of the mud-painted faces of dancers heralding the King of winter's dark entrance into the world of lights … Catherine Hallmark felt a pang in her heart: her solstice party was also her birthday do, and Beatrice, her daughter, was still missing. The planet had changed axis, it seemed, and no matter what the science said, the dark winter had come sooner this year. The atmosphere was free-spirited however, as she had wanted it to be.

The *crème de la crème* of Eden Borough had been invited to witness her metamorphosis into the Winter Queen. Catherine, the ever-young chrysalid, flaunted her full span of wings, like the dragon they always thought she was. For the occasion, she had had a Botox injection and her pouty lips looked like two buoys marooned on sandy ripples. She was determined to put on a show for her admiring guests no matter the odds. Drawing inspiration from William Blake's Great Red Dragon, she finally decided to go for St Michael's to better express the rise and fall of humanism, and for that purpose had had her hairdresser fashion her hair in two large goat horns, based on a painting by Albrecht Durer.

The flamboyance of her décor equalled her costume. Glass chandeliers inundated the festival hall of her twelve-room mansion with bright and sparkling light. The guests marvelled at some of Banksy's art, displayed on the walls of her mansion. Most were prints, she admitted, but one in particular, the original sketch of Ziggy Stardust Elizabeth had been gifted to her by the artist himself, she boasted.

- 'Oh, I know him very well. He's a dear friend of mine,' Catherine pandered to her guests, in her best received pronunciation, her hand fanned across her chest, her eyes closed in humble half-moons, arguing her patronage had made numerous artists famous.

Since Jonathan had come back from his Japanese expedition, her parties had doubled in intensity:

- 'And my nephew has set eyes on the most precious flower in the world. He is here with us today. Where is he? Jonathan? Ah, here you are!' said Catherine.

Catherine grabbed her nephew by the waist, rolling her "r's" emphatically as she bestowed her pedigree on her audience. The rounding guests were now huddling to hear the philantropist's speech.

- 'Jonathan, would you be a darling and tell us what you saw during your expedition?' (more rounding of lips and gasping among the gathering crowd)
- 'Not at all, I saw nothing, but I can tell you that none of the members of the expedition will ever receive any honour for the sacrifice they made. Unfortunately, we have left their bodies to rot in a cave, on the other side of the world, that no one wants to hear about,' said Jonathan.

The crowd gasped.

- 'Oh, well, Jonathan has a peculiar way of diminishing his exploits. I am sure most travellers will recognize in his fortitude the true iron of adventurers,' said Catherine.

The crowd sighed. Catherine resumed her Diva pose:

- 'Dear, oh, dear, what was it like really, just tell us in your own words!' Catherine encouraged Jonathan to speak to the crowd amassed to hear about his adventure.

Catherine expected the guests to applaud her inflappable dauntlessness, but Jonathan had already walked off towards the bar to get a drink:

- 'When my nephew is ready to talk, Oh, I have no doubt we'll have a blast listening to his tales about the Everblue. Watch this space!' She peacocked to the crowd before leaving centre stage with a flourish of wings.
- 'What on earth were you thinking? We talked about this, didn't we?' Catherine admonished.
- 'Never mind the bollocks about your show, Auntie,' said Jonathan.
- 'I say!'

She left him at the bar to cater for her guests and unveil the center piece of her soirée: a painting by Herbert, her gigolo.

- 'Ladies and Gentlemen, I present to you the barnacle's incrustations!' said a page, dressed in a silver scales suit and a mermaid's tail. Long black eyelashes covering her face.
- 'I'd happily put that in my toilets,' said the same voice in the crowd, traceable to a rotund man in a white tuxedo, wearing large glasses rimmed with sparkling diamonds.

Six months had passed since the slaughter. Jonathan sat at the bar in his accustomed somber mood, his head still full of the fury of Mount Asahi. He still felt the drilling wound in his stomach, a strange burning that only abated once he had resumed his dependance on the sweet and smokey scotch galore, before it made it worse.

- 'Pissed off with the pomp, hey?' said Jake.
- 'Oh, you know Jake, I owe you my life, buddy, but there's one life that is dearer than mine. You know who I'm talking about, don't you,' said Jonathan.
- 'I am sure she is somewhere in Tibet, hanging her trousers to dry at the window of some old shack as we speak, living among gipsies or some nomad tribe!
- I doubt it, Jake. We would have heard from her by now.'

Jonathan could not repress the incendiary pain that gnawed at his heart.

- 'She'll never come back.
- She will, John, she will, you'll see!'

While Aunt Catherine paraded her costume to the soirée dedicated to her lover's art and the tale of the Everblue, a nazi flag was rolled down in great pomp across the hall. Guests were agasp. In the middle of the swastika, a blue flower had been schematized as a lotus.

Jonathan couldn't ignore his internal monster of shame and passion, which scotch whiskey didn't seem to edulcorate: shame for dragging the beautiful Beatrice into the hellhole of the Everblue grotto, and passion for the girl he always loved. The scars on his arm reminded him of the plague of the bot fly whose larvae ate at his flesh while he was complacently chasing glory. Every now and then, he still felt the sensation of worms crawling under his skin, insinuating their way into his flesh. The visible traces of their passage reminding him he had been a possessed man all along. And now, six months after the expedition, his demonic ambition was coming back to haunt him.

- 'Sometimes, I'd just wish I'd followed my guts and stayed behind to watch over her,' said Jake, compassionately.
- 'It simply doesn't make sense asking those questions any more,' said Jonathan.
- 'I sure can better see in my heart now,' said Jake, prophetically.
- 'Oh yeah?
- Yes, I think I do.
- Well, go on tell me, Jake, for God's sake! I sure would like to hear it!
- We are nothing but toys in the hands of love …Easy does it, Jake, hey? I mean, that's lame in the way of famous last words, don't you think!
- Wouldn't you say, John? I don't know if love is the key to the mystery anymore.
- Well, it's either that or the fancies of an old dowager.
- Fuck, you're right!' said Jonathan chortling.

The guests were now dancing and revolving in their ballroom dresses and tuxedos at the behest of Catherine Hallmark, whose seventieth birthday promised to be yet another bacchanalian carousal. But Jonathan and Jake could only see skeletons and cadavers rolling in each other's arms, beaming with vanity and condescending oblivion.

Lest We Forget Walden

Jonathan settled in his garden osier armchair. March was round the corner. The phantomatic presence of his aunt left no doubt as to the direction the world had taken since he came back from the Everblue expedition.

He opened the Times paper left by his nurse Gene and browsed the Internet for Scottish news instead, his laptop screen turned against the mid-morning sun. Before he knew it, he was ranting in concert with the editorial line of the Scottish terriers of journalism: Albanese invasion, pension fund syphoned by US investors, debt spirals, corpse-fertilised grain harvest, climate exchange rates, Long-Covid chickens … It was all a blur and it didn't take long before he was fed-up with the news as usual.

"Human nature comes with a sinking feeling," thought Jonathan, "you're either a fish in the pond or the pond itself" … Against space travel fortunes squandered, however, it seems the objectification of women had taken a giant leap backwards. Martians could be satisfied. End-of-line anti-fashion statement leggings signified the end of unwanted solicitation and the return of yoga housewives to the streets.

Jonathan's vigour had been in the hands of such a modern Amazon shopper, the curly ginger-haired Gene, since his discharge from hospital. As she painstakingly emulsified his interest with alacrity and feminine tenderness, he found release in her vocal presence. It wasn't the first time his ego was bulging out of his conscience. Even in her organic mission, he had found her to be duplicitous for a reason he had not been able to fathom until today. Only a few months ago, she still called him Mr. Deadstone. Impressed by his recovery from cancer and his resourcefulness, he had persuaded himself that they had become friends and lovers. His leukemia regressing, his fondness for the angel of the NHS grew inch by inch …Since his return from his Japanese expedition, the cancer had gradually receded and within the last few months, Jonathan was discharged from hospital, put under a home care plan by his insurance and ministrated by Gene's fairy powers under the watchful eye of providence.

To her credit, Gene Switzel was a conscientious nurse who never missed an opportunity to pull Jonathan down a peg or two should his sardonic outlook interfere with her wartime efforts:

- 'What now, Mr. Deadstone, hey?' she asked, wittingly.
- 'I guess I'll see you more regularly, in a less formal capacity,' he joked, looking down at her from his armchair.

Gene was overly-dedicated. He couldn't deny she was a stellar cocksucker who had climbed the ladder of his affection to realms he would never have imagined possible after his infatuation with Beatrice. The height of the pandemic had created the right climate for their sexual attraction to flourish, just as in those war stories of fortitude and dignity. He would sometimes applaud Gene on his doorstep after her visits. But Gene Switzel thought that he was being cynical today, standing on his doorstep. Little did she know why …During the past months, Jonathan had regained enough of his clarity of mind and spirit to uncover Gene Switzel's real motives behind her zealous nursing mantra. Now that his faculties had returned to optimal levels, he understood why she, a thirty-year old Venus, took an interest in a fifty-year old retired shrink with PTSD. After some online research on her LinkedIn account, he became aware that she had connections with the Trinity College, and by extension, Jim Walden, one of the suitors for the golden fleece of the Everblue.

He had not heard of him since the Emigration Inn in Eden Borough. Now, it was all too obvious that his reprieve would only be short-lived. The Everblue recalled him to the promise he had made to Dubois.

God knows what happened to his ashes, he wondered mockingly, watching Gene roaring away in her hybrid Hyundai. He wished Dubois was still around to see what a shitshow the Everblue expedition had come to:

- 'It would serve him well,' he muttered to himself.

Dubois had made it his alma mater to save the world from biological warfare, which the Covid pandemic had brought to awareness. The man-made virus only meant that governments around the world were resorting to extreme measures to control overpopulation and counter-check each other's claims to supremacy. It seemed they were controlling the narrative the best way they could by getting their ducks in a row before the final showdown. Dubois's genuine hope had been to deliver the world from its self-devouring madness by gifting the nations with the wisdom of the Everblue. Now, as usual, governments around the world imposed their cradle-to-grave democracies, while the opium of the people was delivered in syringes with an Oxford Ivy label.

The Chinese were buying up dollar currency faster than the US federal reserve could handle and it seemed that post-pandemic, their 0 Covid policy exposed the true intents of the Eastern world: to disrupt supply chains and torpedo western economies who were fearful of their competition, punishing their post-war reconstruction efforts with blockades and tariffs. Escalation seemed irreversible ...

Jonathan had felt inspired when Dubois entrusted him with the mission to bring back enlightenment to the world. He had flattered himself that Dubois must have thought him deserving enough to carry his torch of humanism. Dubois had made everyone feel the whole expedition was as simple as a stroll in a field of buttercups and red clover in summer. Jonathan had been chosen to continue his legacy in the natural order of things. At least, his leukemia had receded. Far from him the thought that Beatrice could have been the chosen one. Yet, he couldn't dismiss his survivor's guilt now.

Dubois had wanted nothing more than for the Everblue to be protected and that is why he had sought Jonathan's botanical and psychiatric know-how, he had convinced himself, so that he could translate the message of the flower in a language that modern minds could understand.

What if Dubois had been in cahoot with the Trinity College all along? He had felt imbued with his new worldly mission to save humanity from madness. How could he possibly look Beatrice in the eyes again, knowing he had been fooled by the malevolent forces of technocratic Christianism?

In Japan, he had made all the necessary arrangements for Dubois' corpse to be burnt, contrary to the French anthropologist's wishes that it should be gifted to scavengers. But it's not until recently that he made the connection between Dubois's last wishes and the myth of Prometheus. Now with time on his hands, the recovering cancer patient had ample opportunity to brush up on his mythology and the symbolism he had once skimmed through as a student psychiatrist. Prometheus, a Greek semi-God had angered the boss, Zeus, for making humans with clay and fire in his spare time. The punishment for Prometheus's transgression was for his liver to be eaten over and over again by birds of prey. It seemed that Gene Switzel, like him, was also a Stymphalian bird, picking at the sacred wound in order to extract the location of the Everblue for the Trinity College to provide the world with their final solution and take all the glory.

"Fuck her," he thought "and fuck Jim Walden, they won't use me, I will use them!"

So now, he could see why the bubbly nurse had become closer to him. For a reason that he ignored until today, she had insinuated her insightful femineity into his life with unflappable dedication and skillful vicariousness for one reason, and one reason only. Men like him had a sense of duty ... His indebtedness to Gene's moist lingerie and her golden treasure had temporarily relieved him of his sanity, but it was now time to reclaim his lucidity.

"Fuck all that," he thought.

He had done the best he could given the circumstances and his love for Beatrice was real. Why couldn't a man his age have feelings for a young lass? Since when did feelings of love have to be reasonable? *Fuck the guilt, too* ...He could still take up his role in the wild goose chase now that Jim Walden was honing on the Everblue to scavenge some glory. How much did the trinitarian prelate really know? It certainly wasn't Doherty's head that told him. Could he not use the Trinity's momentum to his advantage to find Beatrice after all?

'*You're paranoid*,' had argued Doherty, as the two men discussed what to do with Dubois's body under their care, while the pandemic prevented the flying doctors from reaching the rocky plateau, on Mount Asahi. Gene had also thought him paranoid when he told her about the pandemic being man-made. But what the fuck did they know anyway?

Fuck all that, thought Jonathan. Everything Gene had said to ingratiate herself could now be given in evidence. Jim Walden was back in the picture to find the location of the Everblue now that the hard work had been done and was using Gene to get to him.

As he noticed his fly was open, waving at Gene on his doorstep, he decided that he would contact Jim Walden directly to discuss with him the modalities of a new expedition.

Jonathan had always imagined that Dubois deliberately meant to send a message with his corpse. It all made sense now ... Doherty literally lost his head and his spiritual legacy spoke for itself, and him, who still had his, was decidedly intent on using it. 'Conspiracy theories aren't good for your moral,' Gene had said repeatedly during her visits. But as the darkness of February descended upon his manor house, and the titles of the press dissolved in his visual memory, Jonathan was more than ever set on finding out what had happened to Beatrice at the top of Tomurauchi mountain, and he was now in fine fettle to do so. The Everblue had worked its magic and his will had returned home. It was time to unleash the Everblue hell on those who depreciated humanity to better serve their self-destructive desires on spiritually-hungry crowds …

Moments of Lucidity

The repressive civil servants jives bounced off his ego. Try as he might, Jim Walden couldn't deter Jonathan from his new mission: to find what had happened to Beatrice once and for all. If that involved using the Trinity College's resources, so be it. Jonathan had finally asked Gene to put him in contact with Jim Walden after he exposed their machination. It's the least she could do.

The conference call lasted two hours. Gene Switzel stood by Jonathan, in the lounge of his Scottish mansion, in Eden Borough. She had just finished her day's work and had settled for the night. Now exposed in her scheme, snared in her own trap, Gene was obedient and would vicariously mediate for Jonathan. Jim Walden needed him to find the Everblue, and this year, as last year, spring time was the moment or never to find it. And Jonathan needed Walden to find Beatrice. So why not join forces, he had decided, eating his humble pie, pretending he was acting for the sake of convenience. Of course, Beatrice came up in the conversation after one hour into the call, as Jim Walden now knew the intimate details of their previous expedition:

- 'And what did you do to try and find her after her disappearance?' said Walden.
- 'We looked for three weeks for her on the mountain and down in the towns and villages. The police and rescue people came back with an empty bag. I had to go back because of my health, I was being treated for cancer, remember?' said Jonathan, indignated.
- 'And she was never found?'
- Evidently.
- What do you think happen, Deadstone?' said Walden in his idiosyncratic mellifluous tone of due diligence.

- 'I'd ever know … Not a clue! According to Jake, my sidekick and saviour, she was abducted by an American named Jackson or Taylor, possibly acting out of an occult motive in service of a cult led by Doherty, the psychospiritual guru. He had been harassing her since Yokohama, I believe. But those nutters are incommunicado. The police are still investigating their whereabouts … An American, you say?
- Yes, Doherty's disciple … It's not like you didn't know the sycophantic prelate fancied himself as a Master guru, now, did you?'

Jonathan's anger barometer flared while Walden maintained a placid mien.

- 'Oh, yes, we had information in that regard,' said Walden, now on his guard.
- 'But of course, you did,' said Jonathan, portentously. 'You knew because Doherty was your guy, wasn't he? He was spying for you all along, wasn't he?'

Walden went on mute. At the other end of the line, he had side-tracked Jonathan's remark pretexting some "urgent" conversation with a colleague.

- 'Can you hear me, Walden?' said Jonathan.

There was no answer from Walden, who continued his side conversation …

- 'And the Covid virus jabbed into Chinese meat to make it look like it came from them, were you in on it too? Was the butterfly effect part of the equation too? Are you listening, you fucking Nazis? Were the elderlies who died part of your narrative too? Was your Covid Hiroshima part of the big picture of saving the world too, hey? Is that why they sent their macaque rhesus monkeys to the rescue? What was the plan behind all that, in the end, Walden? Killing two birds with one stone, overpopulation and Asian competition? Delaying climate change action? Making it look like it came from above? What was it all about those economic blockades and sanctions? Did you do your due diligence on that too?' ranted Jonathan.
- 'Jonathan, you're on mute,' said Gene.

- 'Sorry, you were on mute, Dr. Deadstone. What was that?
- I am saying that I didn't embark on this expedition to carry your water, Walden, you and your intelligence-gathering bullshit! Lives were taken during that expedition, cannon fodder was spent, Walden, do you hear me?' Jonathan wobbled with tears.
- 'This is a slight worry,' said Walden, now facing his camera again.
- 'A slight worry? Wh … ? I mean, from an administrative point of view …That's quite a way to put it, and what do you mean by "administrative point of view"?' said Jonathan, grinding his teeth.
- 'I know how painful her disappearance must be for you right now. And I do apologize if I came across a bit flippant, it wasn't my intention, Dr. Deadstone. What I mean is that there were two deaths and a disappearance during the last expedition. I am merely trying to weigh the chances of the College willingness to risk more lives,' said Walden, placatory.

The silent tension on both sides of the line was suddenly palpable.

- 'So why sneak through the back door, sending a nurse to my house in order to extract information, you asshole!' said Jonathan.

Jim Walden was undeterred. His civil service detachment was to be expected. Jonathan wasn't disconcerted in the least either.

- 'Let's not inflame the debate … It was a coincidence. Gene and I go way back. She had never heard about the Everblue before meeting you and her appointment as your nurse had nothing to do with us. It just so happens she worked for us in the past, in her capacity as a practitioner. She reached out later when you started talking to her about the Everblue. Her Google search was flagged by our intelligence gathering service. It was pure coincidence. We have our eyes on more important targets, Dr. Deadstone. For example, the fact that Japan has already developed a chip that can transform CO_2 into spirit matter. The Middle-Eastern countries are potential buyers. It's probably why Taylor and Doherty were over there … '

Jonathan smiled like an automat, the corners of his mouth raised dubitatively.

- 'What? Are you sure it wasn't to relieve the world of its conscience after the pharmaceutical reboot? You're full of it, aren't you, Walden? And who is that moron Doherty supposed to have been working for, Nasa, the military?
- We'll be in touch, Jonathan. My regards Gene!'

Gene said Goodbye to Walden. She was shuddering. Her ginger hair curls jolting in tempo with her spasms, she looked at Jonathan with an air of contrition. Jonathan had recently been diagnosed with a nervous condition called Guillain-Barré, the result of his Covid vaccine:

- 'I am sorry ... I didn't know what to do. Walden pays the bills. I had no choice,' said Gene.
- 'Oh, I'm sorry too ... You were just doing your job, I know. I struggle to see what the Everblue achieved at all,' sobered Jonathan, holding his head in his hands, glancing at his overdue wheelchair.
- 'But, you're rid of leukaemia, that's a bonus, surely?' said Gene, gently taking his hand into hers.
- 'I am ready to go back. I would appreciate your presence as a nurse and a companion, if you are willing,' said Jonathan, decisive.
- 'I am sure the College will find a way to get us through the Military and the official border checks. We may even be accompanied by the local Japanese police,' she said, trying to hold Jonathan's sobering head above water.
- 'I must go back! I'll find a way ... I just need to know what happened to her!' he said.

During the evening, Gene and Jonathan had sex in the sofa, when Gene's knee found the remote control. The news bulletin came on as they both laughed:

- 'Since Everblue flowers have been planted across North Korea, it seems that the one North Koreans dutifully call the Supreme Leader has engaged in a world-wide tour of peace and well-wishing, offering visitors from abroad the opportunity to stay all expenses paid in His

Supreme Excellency's country. Elsewhere, in Japan, China and the eastern territories of Russia, the Everblue appears to attract thousands of pilgrims. The US have come clean on their biological warfare campaigns in China and the latter's premier has publicly forgiven Uncle Sam, promising to align their trade tariffs with the rest of the world.'

Gene turned around to listen more carefully at the TV news bulletin. She scooted on Jonathan's lap, letting herself free of his hold to fetch a bowl of popcorn sitting on the table.

- 'Did you hear that? They are talking about the Everblue on TV?' she said.
- 'That was intense,' said Jonathan, covering his genitals.
- 'Yes, it was! Sorry, I just heard them speak about the Everblue, on TV. I thought you would want to know,' said Gene.

Jonathan sprang to his feet and ran to the bathroom. Gene watched his buttocks wobbling as he trotted back in his underpants. She sat deeper into the sofa, covering her body with a plaid, in anticipation of a follow-up on the topic of the Everblue in the six o'clock news, but the coverage had moved on to strikes around the country …

- 'Rishi Sunak has declared a state of emergency,' commented the newsreader.
- 'What did you hear exactly?' asked Jonathan, prone against the kitchen worktop in his pants.
- 'I heard that the Everblue was in Russia,' said Gene.
- 'Russia? How extraordinary!'
- You said it!
- Are the Trinity College chartering tourists? Is that what it is?
- Ukrainians, it seems, are now planting seeds instead of fighting …Did they mention the Trinity College? I am sure they already set up charities all over the world to oversee the whole process,' said Jonathan, sardonic.
- 'John, it doesn't have to be the College every time there's a catastrophe around the world. And it's not even a catastrophe, it's great news, so why the long face?

- I believe! I believe, I do … Let's dine out tonight to celebrate!' said Jonathan.

Jonathan and Gene took a shower together to make good on their orgasm interrupted by the news. The steaming shower room left no ambiguity as to the joy that the Everblue apparition around the world had brought to Jonathan. At the Sicilian restaurant, Jonathan's favourite, the couple indulged in octopus, meatballs and a bottle of the finest Catarrato:

- 'I knew it! You know what that means, don't you?' said Jonathan, ecstatic.
- 'Beatrice?
- Yes, she's alive! God, this octopus is good, so tender! I still can't figure out how she did it, though.'

With a thumbs up, Jonathan congratulated the chef whose open kitchen was right behind Gene.

- 'Beatrice is not only alive but kicking it down the road! Gosh, I would give anything to know how she collected the seeds. It can't be otherwise. How she went around the snake, and … '

But Jonathan stopped his exuberant scenario in its track.

- 'What is it?' asked Gene, holding a glass of wine mid-air to her lips.
- 'What if it wasn't the Trinity College who took her away? What if it was the flower that had warned her against coming into the cave? What if … I have been dreaming! We have been dreaming all along!' he said, frozen in a prophetic pose, his eyes browsing the business of the kitchens, his fork hanging loosely at the end of this arm, as if he was listening to some distant music.
- 'Now, I am beginning to see,' said Jonathan.
- 'It sounds great either way, she's alive and that's what matters,' said Gene, tempering his excitement with a gentle stroke on his forked hand.
- 'I must contact Jake, as soon as possible! We're only ten days away from our trip and we might need to cancel!

- What trip?' said Gene, worried.

Jonathan evaded her question. He had not told her that he had been planning another trip to Japan with Jake.

- 'Your face is beaming with hope all of a sudden, you look ten years younger!' said Gene.
- 'Do I? I am sure she will come back to us soon, that's why. She just had some important world-saving to do on her way back, that's all,' said Jonathan, radiating with hope.

Jake remained authentically autistic in his urban casual hipster gear. But with the added benefit of the flower's wisdom in his smile and the prerogative of youth travel behind him, sitting on one of Eden Borough's art gallery's wooden bench, Jonathan heard how Jake Edwards-Angst had spread the news about Beatrice being a missing person on social media … At first, he had little ambition the message would spread beyond his immediate friends. Since he always knew she was fine, his campaigns had enabled Doctors without borders to trace her deeds to Tibet, as he had suggested. He had contacted the Dalai Lama on Twitter. Beatrice was not of this world anymore, he was told, but could be reached through the intercession of priests. Another Buddhist sect reached out to let Jake know of her whereabouts in the parallel world of spirits. Not only had she become a spiritual entity, he told Jonathan, but she had been the one to make it to the flower's heart during the expedition led by Hashita. She had surrendered to the flower in what Jake was trying to describe was a parallel universe.

- 'What do you mean by parallel?' said Jonathan, puzzled.
- 'The Dalai Lama told me that her spirit was moving places, but she was nowhere to be found in the physical world, basically. None of what we went through happened to Beatrice whose experience was totally different! That's what I mean, and it's easy to understand really. She never went missing! I mean, she was missing in our world, but not hers!
- Run it through me again, Jake … I've been living in this world for a good fifty years now. I need time to get it round my head. Plus, I'm driving now … '

As Jonathan laid his phone on his lap, he fumbled for the speaker button. Jonathan was driving back to his mansion, listening to Jake's excited account of his discovery of Beatrice's parallel world.

- 'You must come to Eden Borough, Jake. I want to hear the whole story. I want to understand exactly how this happened and I am sending a car to pick you up. You don't even have to worry about travel arrangements. Let me organise everything!'

Jake arrived at Eden Borough's station twenty minutes behind schedule. He was expecting to see a car waiting for him, someone with a placard with his name on it or something similar. Instead, an old man in his early eighties was waiting by the entrance. He was the only one there apparently. The old man's double-breasted Trench coat looked shabby but uncreased, and his head was bowed, as if he was sleeping, like an old nag on two feet.

- 'Excuse me, are you waiting for me?' said Jake.
- 'Hm?'

The old man raised his head slowly and revealed two yellow beady eyes where a faint hue of blue could be seen behind square thin-rimmed glasses. His thin neck seemed to have disappeared behind his grey striped tie. His shirt the same colour as the whites of his eyes:

- 'Dr. Deadstone sent you?
- Yes sir, I was waiting for you. This way, please,' said the old man's flimsy voice.

The elderly chauffeur shuffled like a snail towards the exit, his arms balancing like an alpine skier on a trekking slope, only hundred times slower … Jake tiptoed behind him, afraid he might wake up at any moment, trying to reassure himself that Jonathan would never have sent him his chauffeur if he didn't trust his driving abilities. Or so he hoped, his mind bustling with catastrophic scenarios. Jake sat the back, while the old man sat in the front passenger seat …

- 'Excuse me, said Jake, who's driving?
- You drive,' said the old man, even-tempered in his posture and voice.
- 'I can't drive! What ... ?
- Okay.'

The old man got out of the car, walked round the bonnet and sat in the driving seat, looking straight ahead. They finally left the station and the car park, following an A road out of Eden borough. The chauffeur never once looked in the interior mirror. The journey to his manor house would last about twenty minutes, had said Jonathan. As soon as they left the town and its suburbs, the country side became stubbornly dark and deeply carved by a shadowy landscape. The rocky face along the country roads hid most of the sea side views, but on the opposite side of the road, as soon as they left town, a vast forest of pines seemed to unravel for ever through Jake's window. He soon fell asleep as the old man's driving was as smooth as a bullet train ...

- 'Sir, we are here,' said the old driver.

The door opened and the old man held it for Jake who could not tell at first if he was still dreaming. Jonathan opened the door and the light pierced the veil over his drowsy eyes:

- 'Come in, old chap! I have a wee twenty-year-old scotch for you to get your juices running,' said Jonathan.

Jonathan looked over his shoulder while he was walking Jake to his study. Jake looked around and recognized the interior, which he had seen once with Beatrice a couple of years before.

- 'I know how dreary William can be. I have often wished he was less predictable.
- Sorry for being late, you'd think they'd make an excuse for the trains running behind schedule. I don't know why trains are never on time, except to while away terrorists or something!
- No chance of finding an explanation for trains being late, they stopped talking a long time ago, those puffing billies, Jake.'

Jake sat down in a large cow horn chair covered with red velvet upholstery.

- 'Are these for real?
- What, the horns? Yes sure … They came with the house.
- Oh, yes, the MacLeods!' said Jake.
- 'That's right … So, Jake, what exciting news, hey?' Jonathan let out a frank and elated sigh.
- 'It sure is!' Jake agreed.
- 'But before you must explain to me this parallel world you spoke of! How do you account for the Sherpa's disappearance too? No one ever heard from him again, did they?
- Well, I have my theory, John.'

Jake proceeded to explain how it could have been that Beatrice was in fact the only one who had truly been in contact with the flower. For the rest of the expeditionists, the grotto had only been an illusion …

- 'An illusion, Jake? Do you remember your slashed hands, my heart attack on the mountain? It seems like you've developed a very selective memory recently, wouldn't you say?'

Jonathan poured Jake a large glass of his vintage Bladnoch.

- 'Yes, I thought so too …Gosh, you have aged well in two years, how old are you now?
- Twenty-three.
- Oh, my god, don't let him bottle you in! He's a master craftsman at distilling your nerves, that old fox!' said a voice from the doorframe.
- 'Who is?' said Jonathan.
- 'Well, let's say time is not on his side any more,' said Gene.

Gene barged in the study. Jake watched her fiery ginger robe incensing the room.

- 'Ah! I have a lot more to give to this world, Gene, don't be sassy! Give us another hour or two, we're catching up on old times! Are you hungry Jake, do you want a sandwich or something? Ham, cheese, pickles?' said Jonathan.
- 'Thank you, I'd love one,' said Jake.
- 'Gene, do you know Jake? If you don't, he's the one who saved my life on the mountain!
- Of course, I've heard a lot about you,' said Gene, holding her hand out.

Gene stroke Jake's shoulder and gave him a kiss on the cheek. Her fluid lines and cheering sparkle radiated through Jake's spine. Jonathan sat in his study armchair and brought it closer to the fire as Gene left the room.

- 'So, what you're saying is that Beatrice is the one who actually saw the flower? But we didn't? That we dreamt? Is that what you're saying?' asked Jonathan, crossing his long legs in the armchair, his head slightly tilted. Jake saw his jaws tightening into a square, impenetrable vice of curiosity. Of course, Jonathan had his own theory, but Jake's enlightened autism would certainly bring water to his mill.
- 'No, not exactly … We lived through the same events, but I think we didn't actually see the real flower, but an imaginary clone. Do you remember how the sherpa disappeared?
- Y … es?
- This is your clue. Let me … Because the sherpa was not among us when we approached the flower, it tells you that it wasn't real.
- How is that a certainty for you?' asked Jonathan, looking down his glass, probing Jake's version of events thoughtfully.
- 'The Sherpa was the most neutral, less interested party among us. He had shown no signs of being overly excited or even interested in the flower itself. For him, as you remember, it was just another job, right?
- Okay, I see what you're getting at. He would have disappeared because his mind wasn't in the game, and therefore it tells us that it was a spell, some sort of mind trick that fooled us only because we were hooked, some triage that the flower orchestrated, or the spirit thereof … A bit like this scotch whiskey with our blood oxygen! Yes,' laughed Jake. 'Ah, I'm so happy Beatrice is found again! I so missed her!'

Jonathan nodded with empathy:
- 'I am so relieved too, but if what you say is true, we'll never see her again,' he said bluntly.

Jake looked at Jonathan who had become suddenly sombre and pensive.

- 'What is it?' asked Jake, hesitant.
- 'Oh, hm, nothing, some stupid lapsus, hm, a random neuronal connection, it's been happening quite a few times recently.
- Oh … Sorry to hear that, but what do you mean, John?
- Have you had any signs or symptoms of a disturbance yourself, Jake?'

Gene walked in with the sandwich, two large rustic loaves of bread and a thick slice of honeyed ham hock spread with mustard and pickles.

- 'Wow, thanks!' said Jake.
- 'Do you want crisps with it?' said Gene.
- 'Oh … ' Jake hesitated, out of politeness.
- 'Of course, he does, who wouldn't want crisps with ham and mustard? An alien from Mars, maybe?' said Jonathan.

Gene walked out again …

- 'You and Gene are …We are good friends, yes, and lovers … Good? I don't know, I think so. But, what about this sherpa, then? Where is he now, in a parallel world too?' asked Jonathan.

Jake was munching and swallowing down as fast as he could, but the food morsels were larger than his throat could handle.

- 'Take your time, Jakey … I'm gonna tell you something now … To anyone listening to this conversation, it might seem terribly menacing, but we are not of this world anymore.
- 'I agree!' said Jake, to please Jonathan. 'Er … What???'

While Gene lay the bowl of crisps on the small mahogany table between the oriental pouch and the flowers crib drying by the fire, they both looked at Jake whose incredulous eyes interrogated them alternatively. His mouth was open on a bolus of ham and cheese.

- 'It's as if what we're hearing about the world, right now, is fake, but also true because we are living it,' said Jonathan, clarifying for Jake's sake.
- 'Exactly, it's like Williams' driving,' said Jake, now tuned in.
- 'Exactly! But it's an illusion and God knows when or where we'll wake up!' said Jonathan.
- 'What are you talking about you two?' said Gene, arms akimbo.

They both looked at each other and nodded.

- 'We have to go back and confront our fears, my boy. Go back to where it all started,' said Jonathan.

Jonathan stood up and pushed the homeopathic flower crib aside. His pussy willow blooms felt downy, felt-like to the touch.

- 'Let me show you something, Jake,' said Jonathan, brusquely standing up.

Jake followed Jonathan along solid coffered pine walls, carved with grape motifs and varnished by years of passage. Jonathan put his hand on a newel post to rest.

- 'I'm still recovering and my orthostatic pressure is iffy, but I'm free of leukaemia now, Jake.
- Thoroughly glad to hear it, John. I didn't want to believe it on the phone.
- Here. This is the secret MacLeod's vault!

Jonathan pushed a secret panel and opened the door onto his vault.

- Seriously?' Jake's open jaws felt like a satisfying flourish to Jonathan's hat trick when he opened the secret door to the white enamel tiled vault where wooden shelves held various artefacts.
- 'This is the vault where a few years ago, I discovered another secret room, you see …A secret room within the secret room?
- Yes, and lo and behold!'

Jonathan opened a makeshift door he explained was his making.

- 'I am not a great carpenter, but what matters is what's inside!' said Jonathan, ushering Jake into the vault's secret room.

Jake gawped at the interior of a small cave-like room with a makeshift hammerbeam ceiling. The confined space wasn't lit but he could distinguish a desk with drawers and a wardrobe.

- 'In this desk, you have pre-war and war paraphernalia. Now, look at this!' said Jonathan.

Jonathan produced a translucent plastic bag from one of the miserable desk's drawer, from which he extracted a newspaper clip:

- 'And here's the article about the Everblue … Sic! What does that tell us, Jake?
- I am gobsmacked! Utterly jaw dropping stuff,' said Jake.
- 'But what do you think it means to you and I?'

They both looked at the newspaper clip and crossed eyes, waiting on the other to deduct the obvious.

- 'So, it was real then but not now,' said Jake, tentatively.
- 'It was real, but not in our time, is what you want to say. We must have bifurcated at some point, which means we're living in a parallel reality since we saw the flower's little sister or we have departed from the real world itself! Whichever is the slowest,' said Jonathan, humorously.
- 'So, we were always meant to step in that false reality and never return?

- It's the only possibility …And …Jake, don't say it …So, that's why your face changed all of a sudden when I mentioned the parallel word, right?' said Jake.
- 'Beatrice lives in another world, working for us, but there's little chance we'll ever meet again. We were unchosen, so to say.'

Jonathan left the vault open. He closed the heavy wooden pine door behind them but the secret room was left open in the wake of their memories … In their mind, there would always be the secret possibility that Beatrice could be found again, but none of them wanted to break that thin veil of mystery or discuss it further. Hope is a terrible thing. Each knew exactly what the other was thinking: it was their choice if they wanted to try and gain access to that parallel world that was now open. Whether or not they would be successful was the lock and key mystery to their own soul:

- 'The metaphysics of love is the alchemy of poets, Jake. Remember this door is open and go well,' said Jonathan.

With these words, Jonathan and Jake said goodbye and hugged. They knew they wouldn't see each other for a long time still. There was no need to poke the wound of Beatrice's disappearance again, as they both knew her sacrifice had been the reason why their own world had been saved. The MacLeod's vault, the milky way they both set eyes on once could still inspire them if they wished, but the Everblue had made its choice …In front of Jonathan's mansion, old Williams opened the car door and Jake waved again at Jonathan's fractal silhouette behind the car glaze. He sat comfortably in the old dark blue Morgan once again, his heart beating in his chest for a reason he knew was the making of this new friendship, without being able to put a finger on the "how".

Once Williams slowly parked into the only parking space available in front of the train station where he had picked up Jake, the old man watched his passenger walk unsure-footed, slouched, as he scissor gaited his way into the station, listening to the nightingales chirp away in the setting darkness of the Eden Borough sky.

The old wooden bench of the small rural station felt alive and full of the spirit of the forest glowing around Jake, in the darkness of the rural landscape, as he walked through the gates towards the platforms. He switched on his app and settled his ear phones on his head. Then, he sat down thinking of the wood that made the bench, his mind befuddled, mustard still on his lips, pickles still tantalising his stomach juices ... Suffused with a nervous energy that he could not identify as any particular emotion, he began thinking about his theory and how it had taken a shrink to reverse it like a pancake. The observer influences what is observed, so that nothing is fixed or finite in the grand scheme of things. Still, Jake smiled at the thought of Beatrice lighting fires of joy and hope wherever she went, by virtue of her immense and universal heart ...